The
the

To survive against such overwhelming odds required movement—he would have to run the risk of seeking higher ground.

Holstering the Desert Eagle but keeping hold of his Beretta, Bolan grabbed the mirror extending from the rear corner of the van and pulled himself to the roof of the vehicle, flattening himself against it.

The gunmen would have his range in seconds. He drew his Desert Eagle once more, extended his arms out to each side, and began shooting from the roof of the van. The fusillade pinned the gunmen nearest to the van, striking and wounding some of them, killing still others. But there were more assassins than the soldier had realized.

The cargo van shook beneath him. Men were climbing inside. They would no doubt try to shoot him through the roof.

Bolan beat them to it. Holstering the Beretta and swapping magazines in the Desert Eagle, he aimed at the roof of the van and started pulling the trigger, walking the shots in an ever-widening pattern. Men screamed below him as bodies hit the floor of the vehicle.

He flattened himself again and spun around, shooting left and right, taking running gunmen this way and that.

It was time to move.

MACK BOLAN ®
The Executioner

The Executioner®
Don Pendleton's

FATAL COMBAT

A GOLD EAGLE BOOK FROM
WORLDWIDE®

TORONTO • NEW YORK • LONDON
AMSTERDAM • PARIS • SYDNEY • HAMBURG
STOCKHOLM • ATHENS • TOKYO • MILAN
MADRID • WARSAW • BUDAPEST • AUCKLAND

Recycling programs
for this product may
not exist in your area.

First edition November 2011

ISBN-13: 978-0-373-64396-7

Special thanks and acknowledgment to
Phil Elmore for his contribution to this work.

FATAL COMBAT

Whereat with blade, with bloody blameful blade, / He bravely broached his boiling bloody breast.
—William Shakespeare
1564–1616

There are those who think that killing is a game. There are men who believe the weapons in their hands make them the predators. But the sharpest weapon is the human mind...and the game, when hunting predators, has no rules.
—Mack Bolan

THE
MACK BOLAN
LEGEND

Nothing less than a war could have fashioned the destiny of the man called Mack Bolan. Bolan earned the Executioner title in the jungle hell of Vietnam.

But this soldier also wore another name—Sergeant Mercy. He was so tagged because of the compassion he showed to wounded comrades-in-arms and Vietnamese civilians.

Mack Bolan's second tour of duty ended prematurely when he was given emergency leave to return home and bury his family, victims of the Mob. Then he declared a one-man war against the Mafia.

He confronted the Families head-on from coast to coast, and soon a hope of victory began to appear. But Bolan had broken society's every rule. That same society started gunning for this elusive warrior—to no avail.

So Bolan was offered amnesty to work within the system against terrorism. This time, as an employee of Uncle Sam, Bolan became Colonel John Phoenix. With a command center at Stony Man Farm in Virginia, he and his new allies—Able Team and Phoenix Force—waged relentless war on a new adversary: the KGB.

But when his one true love, April Rose, died at the hands of the Soviet terror machine, Bolan severed all ties with Establishment authority.

Now, after a lengthy lone-wolf struggle and much soul-searching, the Executioner has agreed to enter an "arm's-length" alliance with his government once more, reserving the right to pursue personal missions in his Everlasting War.

The morning air held a tang of moisture that beaded on the windshield as the sun hit it, chasing the crisp October dawn as a pollution-laden haze took its place. Three truant high school kids paused on the sidewalk not far from the parked car, craning their necks for a better look. A uniformed Detroit police officer shooed them away, muttering something about getting to school, and the teens shot back cheerful profanities as they made themselves scarce. The cop, shaking his head, turned back to the chalk outline visible among the milling crime scene team.

There was blood everywhere.

The dried blood, thicker and darker than most civilians would or could imagine, had washed across the crags of the asphalt in an impossibly wide bloom that partially obscured the chalk outline. Solemn figures were loading the zippered body bag in the back of the medical examiner's van. They had seen many corpses; they would be hardened to all but the most brutal of deaths.

Their grim expressions confirmed what the crimson lake of human blood had already told the man behind the wheel.

Mack Bolan, aka the Executioner, dropped the window on the driver's side of the rented Dodge Charger. He put his left hand on the steering wheel and leaned forward for a better look. In his right hand, resting on his leg, was a custom-tuned Beretta 93-R machine pistol.

Satisfied with what he could see from his vantage point, Bolan turned his attention to the weapon. He ejected the well-traveled pistol's 20-round magazine and racked the slide, catching the loose round in his palm. Then he reloaded the round, seated it and racked the slide again, nudging the weapon's selector switch and replacing it in the leather shoulder holster he wore under his three-quarter-length black leather coat. The coat concealed both the .44 Magnum Desert Eagle he wore inside his waistband in a Kydex holster and the double-edged Sting knife he carried in a matching sheath, also in his waistband, behind his left hip, angled for a draw with either hand.

On the seat next to Bolan was an olive-drab canvas war bag. The bag contained a variety of items and gear, including spare magazines and ammunition, grenades, other explosives, and various sundry combat essentials. The Executioner had spent too many years fighting his war, often with very little backup, to walk into the field underprepared. He had pared down his standard mission load-out over that time to make sure he had anticipated every need that could be foreseen. In combat, of course, not all scenarios could be predicted. Still, he was as prepared before fact as was realistic for a soldier to be. The rest was adaptability, flexibility and will.

Even as his mind turned these thoughts over in his head, the Executioner examined the problem before him. The clinical part of his brain filed the data of his senses—the inordinate quantity of blood, the bodily damage needed to produce it, and the public location of the body. These were indicators of the predator who had taken this kill. Another man might call them clues. Bolan was no detective, but he was an expert in predators. He was a soldier and a hunter.

One of the locals, who wore an ill-fitting blazer rather

than a uniform, detached himself from the crowd working the crime scene. He jogged across the blocked street with a manila folder in one hand. Bolan resisted the urge to shake his head. His contact at Stony Man Farm had told him the locals would, on orders through channels, assign to him a liaison within the Detroit PD. That liaison turned out to be one Adam Davis, newly minted detective. The young man wasn't a rookie, but according to his files he hadn't had the time to put much distance between himself and that tag before earning his way out of his uniform.

Davis got into the passenger seat at Bolan's gesture, closing the door behind him and thrusting a file folder at Bolan.

"Agent Cooper," he said. "This is everything so far. They're still working up some of the details."

Matt Cooper was the name on Bolan's Justice Department credentials. He had used the alias often enough that the Cooper cover identity had an impressive history and dossier of its own. Any curious local poking through law-enforcement files would find sufficient detail to compel cooperation with the mysterious agent, whose precise responsibilities in this matter had purposely been left vague.

Bolan took the folder from Davis's hand, watching the man flinch as if he expected the agent to take a few fingers with him. Bolan quashed the urge to shake his head and chuckle. It wouldn't do to antagonize Davis, whose only crime so far was being intimidated by implied authority. Davis was the most junior detective in a department known for its graft and corruption. Faced with a mysterious governmental operative to whom Davis's own superiors were required to give cooperation, what else could he think? He'd find his way readily enough. He had that eager, adaptable air to him. Bolan had encountered the type enough times to recognize it.

The folder contained a preliminary field report. It also held a series of slightly smudged color photos, obviously printed on a portable ink-jet unit and handled with haste. Bolan was accustomed to meeting with resistance from local law enforcement, if only because the usual petty jurisdictional squabbles annoyed those through whose territory the Executioner marched. It was refreshing actually to get some cooperation. He wondered for a moment if Hal Brognola had rattled cages on this end of the situation perhaps a bit more loudly than usual.

Certainly the big Fed had sounded more stressed than was normal even for him, when he placed the scrambled phone call to Bolan's secure satellite phone from Brognola's Justice Department office near the Potomac. The soldier could picture the man chewing an unlit cigar and sitting in front of the window in his chair deep in Wonderland, a fighting bureaucrat waging wars of intrigue, intimidation and political manipulation that even Bolan could not win alone. Brognola was the director of the Sensitive Operations Group, a counterterrorist unit based at Stony Man Farm in Virginia, and on the other end of *his* phone was the Man himself, the President of the United States.

"Striker," Brognola had said, using the soldier's code name. "Somebody's cutting up civilians in Detroit."

Bolan had said nothing for a moment. "I'm listening," he finally answered.

The big Fed wasted no time. "It's been going on for a while, now. So far the press has been kept out of it, but that hasn't been easy, nor can the powers that be contain it any longer. The murders are increasing in frequency and in their public nature. Whoever's doing it has stopped being careful—it's as if he or she wants the bodies found."

"A serial killer?"

"Possibly," Brognola said. "Officially there are no leads. Unofficially, and very strictly off the record at this point, the Man is concerned that this isn't a domestic crime at all, but rather a new kind of terrorism."

"Low budget," Bolan said. "Low-tech. Inspire fear by making the populace believe no one is safe."

"Exactly," Brognola said. "If it is a terrorist group, they're destabilizing the greater Detroit area by making its citizens believe the general public, individually, is being targeted. It wouldn't be the first time an international terror ring has used knives to make its bloody business known. The Detroit PD and the FBI have been working to keep this from going off the rails, but they're out of their depth. There are too many rules, too many bureaucratic hurdles, and no way to find or target the enemy. They simply aren't equipped to fight this kind of war."

"But I am," Bolan said. It was not a question.

"The Man wants you to do what you do, Striker," Brognola said. "If Detroit is a test case for some new, insidious campaign, you will root it out and destroy it before it goes any further. You're also working against the clock."

"How so?"

"The Detroit papers are ready to break the story," Brognola said, frustration clear in his voice. "The locals, the FBI, and even Justice have been sitting on them over the last two days…but they're screaming freedom of the press, and honestly, Striker, I can't blame them. We have it on good authority that they're breaking the story the night of October 31, in prime time, which means you're going to have a full-blown panic on your hands before nightfall."

"Which will make it harder to bring my targets to ground," Bolan said.

"Yes," Brognola said. "There's nothing we can do."

"I'll deal with it," Bolan said.

"Hell of a way to kick off Halloween," Brognola said. "You'll have backup among the Detroit PD. I'll lean on the Feds that way, too, and pull as many strings as I have to if you ruffle any feathers."

"You're mixing your metaphors, Hal."

"Whatever," Brognola said. "Striker, I know every mission is important. But this is…different. These are innocent people. Ordinary American citizens. They're being killed for no reason."

A muscle in Bolan's jaw worked. "I haven't forgotten," he said. "I'll get them, Hal."

"Good hunting, Striker."

"On it. Striker out."

With those words, Bolan had stowed his phone and made arrangements to travel to Detroit, where his customary gear had already been prepared and was waiting for him with a Stony Man courier. Now, only a few hours after that conversation, he was here, and he was ready.

It was time to begin.

He was no stranger to Detroit, but he did not know the city like a local. He had been assured that Detective Davis was born and bred here. The Farm had transmitted the man's full dossier to Bolan's phone while he was in transit. He had reviewed it early that morning.

Bolan turned to give the detective a long, hard look. Davis looked up from the manila folder. He reddened. "Uh…sir? Mister, I mean, Agent Cooper, sir? Is there a problem?"

"There might be," Bolan said. "Time for a decision, kid."

"Sir?"

"The department has been instructed to cooperate with me," Bolan said. "There's going to come a moment, not very long from now, when you'll be tempted not to do that."

"I don't understand, Agent Cooper."

Bolan didn't have time for a lengthy argument. He drew the Beretta 93-R from his shoulder holster and placed it in his lap. Davis glanced at it and then did an almost comical double-take. What he had taken for a simple Beretta 92-F pistol was instead a select-fire automatic weapon, and he recognized it as such.

Bolan gave Davis mental points for that.

Next he produced the Desert Eagle, watched Davis's eyes widen at the massive weapon and replaced it. He reholstered the Beretta.

"Sir?"

"Many officers, especially those in smaller cities, go their entire lives without firing their weapons," Bolan said. "In a big, violent city like Detroit, those chances are lower, but still good. Before we're through, there's a very good chance you'll see me fire both of these. And you *will* fire your own weapon. Show me."

Davis hesitated only the barest fraction of a second. He reached into his jacket and then, carefully, withdrew his pistol. He ejected the magazine of the Glock 19 and racked the slide, dropping the ejected round. He hit his head on the dash diving for it, but he got it.

"Spare magazines?" Bolan asked.

"Two, Agent Cooper."

"Well, swing by the station and pick up some spares. That's issue?"

"Department approved list," Davis said.

"All right," Bolan said. "Now. Are you in or out, Davis?"

"Uh… Well, in, of course, sir. I mean, the department assigned."

"No, Davis. You. You personally. We're about to walk down a dark hallway. If you're going to do it, you need to know that it's coming. That it might get bad. That it almost certainly will. Think carefully. I don't want a quick answer. I want to know if you'll stick this out."

Davis looked away. Bolan watched him swallow, hard. He was thinking about it. The subtle change to the set of the younger man's shoulders told the soldier what Davis's answer would be…and that he meant it.

Davis turned to meet Bolan's gaze. "I'm in."

"Good," Bolan said.

"So who are you, Cooper? Really?"

"Like the card says," Bolan said. He reached into his pocket and produced a business card. The front of the card was blank except for the engraved words, *Matt Cooper, Justice Department.*

Davis turned the card over and ran a hand through his thick, close-cropped hair. "These contact numbers?"

"They'll forward to my wireless," Bolan said. "If we get separated, call any of them. You'll reach me no matter what."

Davis nodded. He reached into his jacket. "I have the list your supervisor said you wanted."

Bolan almost smiled at that. The idea of Brognola as anyone's mere "supervisor," perhaps fighting with the photocopier or drinking coffee in a break room, struck him as laughable. He knew precisely what Davis was talking about, however. He had sent the request to the Farm by text message while reviewing the files transmitted to his phone. He needed a place to start, and the murder victims were it.

Innocent people had died, their blood on the knife of some psycho killer…or killers. Government profilers would look for patterns in victims in order to find serial killers. If this was a serial killer, a group of them—it was rare, but it had happened before—the common thread among the victims would tell Bolan where to look next. If there truly was no thread, and the victims were chosen merely for convenience, then looking deeper into the circumstances of their murders would likewise give him something to go on.

Bolan was no detective; he was a battle-hardened, experience-trained soldier. But he understood predators. After witnessing the aftermath of the latest killing, he had no doubt that he was dealing with at least one truly deadly bipedal monster.

The Executioner was going hunting.

"Every victim so far," Davis said, handing over the list, "as tabulated by the folks at the department. You'll find current addresses and, where possible, some notes from the files that seemed relevant. You realize, though, sir, that the killings are apparently random. It's not likely we'll find anything."

"These notes are handwritten," Bolan said, ignoring Davis's other remarks.

"The notes? Yes, sir, Agent Cooper." Davis nodded. "I made them."

Bolan nodded. Initiative even though he thought Agent Cooper was barking up the wrong tree. That was good. It meant Davis wasn't afraid to speak his mind.

He would, however, have to be careful. Brognola hadn't said it out loud; it hadn't been necessary. A group of killers operating for this long, under these conditions, the killings until recently covered up—it reeked of police corruption. Brognola wasn't normally so down on local law enforcement. The fact that he'd spoken so harshly of the men and women on the ground here was a coded message to Bolan, just in case Brognola's words ever went beyond the walls of his office. The man was smart, and he hadn't stayed where he was in the Justice Department for so long without having a few tricks up his sleeves. Assuming the walls had ears was one of these.

"So where do we start, Agent Cooper?"

"At the beginning," Bolan said. "First name on the list. We'll shake the tree and sees what falls loose." There was, of course, the possibility that going back over the territory trod by the killers would make them nervous, bring them out. Depending on how professional they were—a well-financed and trained terrorist cell, for example—this might make little difference. But it might cause something to break. Bolan could feel it; he could see it in the pavement; he could smell it in the air. Things were going to get bloody before it was over.

"I know that neighborhood," Davis said. "It's not exactly one of Detroit's more affluent ones."

"Good thing I've got a cop to go with me," Bolan said.

He put the car into gear and looked up to check the rearview mirror.

He heard the gunshot just as the mirror exploded, pelting him with sharp fragments of plastic and glass.

2

"Down!" Bolan shouted. He stomped the accelerator to the floor, whipping the steering wheel hard over. The powerful engine growled in response, and the Charger burned rubber as it heeled around, pushing Bolan and Davis back in their seats. The detective crouched behind the dash and Bolan did his best to slide, fractionally, into his bucket seat as he urged the car forward, toward the danger. Bullet holes starred the windshield, joining the one that had taken the mirror with it. Bolan ignored them, his right hand clenching the wheel, his left hand snaking into his jacket to reverse-draw the Beretta.

There were at least half a dozen shooters fanned out and moving up the street as if a small army of cops weren't barely within earshot. They wore street clothes and carried themselves with a practiced, almost casual menace that Bolan immediately recognized. These were hired guns, street muscle, and they would have had to be paid well to mount the brazen assault they pushed.

The shooters had automatic rifles, a motley collection of Kalashnikovs, ARs, and other assault weapons. Bullets ripped a path up the hood of the Charger as Bolan crushed the pedal under his boot. He went straight for the lead gunner, a man in a leather jacket who held an AK to his shoulder. He shouted something as Bolan bore down on him.

"Holy—" Davis started to say.

The Charger slammed into the gunman with bone-crushing force. The collision flattened the car's nose, driving its hood under the target's suddenly airborne body. The windshield took the impact after that, turning to glass spiderwebs and blood tracings, jarring Bolan and Davis in their seats. The soldier slammed the Charger into Reverse and burned rubber again, whipping around, the car taking broadsides from the other gunmen. The shooters had been scattered by the Executioner's automotive missile, but they had recovered quickly and were once again pouring on the fire.

Answering shots came from the officers on the scene, as the uniformed contingent recovered from the shock of the attack and began to get into the action. Bolan was grateful but wasn't about to let the Detroit Police Department fight his battle for him. And there was no doubt in his mind that it was his battle, for the attack had been just too coincidental, too seemingly without motive, to be anything other than a hit directed at him personally. Unless Davis had some serious gambling debts Bolan didn't know about, these were killers whose mission was to eliminate Agent Cooper.

As the bullet-riddled Charger spun about, Davis was up in his seat, his Glock in his hand, firing at targets of opportunity. The gunmen weren't hard to spot, bold as they were, standing in full view of God, the Detroit PD and anybody, emptying illegal full-automatic weaponry on a public street. Distant screams told Bolan that the gunfight had caught the attention of the neighbors. But there were no innocents in the line of fire…yet. Bolan knew he would have to end this engagement as quickly as possible to prevent that from changing.

He fired out his window, the Beretta 93-R set for 3-round bursts, punching his enemies in the head whenever possible and going for center-of-mass shots when the angle was poor. The hollowpoint 9 mm bullets did their deadly work as Davis punctuated Bolan's machine pistol blasts with single shots of his own.

Bolan pushed the Charger up onto the narrow sidewalk and between a building and a light pole, drawing sparks and the shrieking of metal on metal from the flank of the tortured rental car. One of the gunmen wasn't fast enough; he fell under the crumpled bumper of the Dodge, causing the vehicle to bounce upward over the speed bump of his sudden corpse. Bolan dug in, accelerating again, causing Davis to grimace as the Charger burned sideways on squealing tires. Davis dropped one more shooter and Bolan punched yet another in the head and neck.

"Who are they?" Davis shouted over the din.

"Hired help," Bolan said, dropping a nearly empty 20-round magazine and swapping it for a fresh one from the pouches in his custom leather shoulder holster. "And they didn't just come from nowhere. Look for a vehicle with passenger capacity, or a cluster of cars."

The Charger's engine was starting to spew black, oily smoke, spraying the wrecked windshield with spurts of oil. Bolan urged it on, shooting across the street, charting a course directly for a man with a MAC-10 submachine gun dressed in dark pants and shirt with a stained trench coat over these. Something about this one, in particular, struck Bolan as familiar—just as the Charger struck its target. A spray of heavy .45-caliber slugs almost chewed through the roof as Davis and Bolan threw themselves to either side. The bullets ripped up the interior of the car and smashed out what was left of the rear window.

Bolan cut short, sharp circles with the car, his jaw set, his eyes roving the crowd and the players running among it, gauging targets of opportunity and screening friendlies from his mental computations. He gripped the wheel with one hand

and fired with the other, the Beretta barking a deadly rhythm. He stroked triple bursts of 9 mm hollowpoint rounds from the snout of the machine pistol, cutting down another, and another, and another gunman. Bodies were beginning to pile up two deep, or so it seemed.

That was an illusion brought on by the adrenaline, the tunnel vision, the tachypsychia of mortal combat. Bolan, while not immune to the physiological effects of life-and-death battle, was certainly no stranger to these sensations. He was as comfortable operating with and through them as it was possible for a human being to be. Still, that did not mean a great deal. Bolan understood, as so many veteran operators did, that much of combat efficacy was simply learning to function efficiently and accurately despite the psychological effects of the fight itself.

Combat was as natural to Bolan as breathing. And he did not think these things, did not subvocalize them, did not consider them as he swapped out another empty 20-round magazine in the Beretta, leaning on the steering wheel with his left knee as he racked the Beretta's slide and chambered the first round.

"Cooper!" Davis yelled. Again Bolan did not think; he did not need to ask. He flattened himself against his headrest and squeezed his eyes shut, tucking his chin, as Davis's Glock came up in his direction.

The shots were deafening in the enclosed space of the Charger's front seats. Davis had seen the man in the leather jacket before Bolan and had responded, as he was trained to do. The gunner held a drum-fed semiautomatic shotgun and managed to scrape the driver's-side fender of Bolan's vehicle with double-00 Buck pellets as he went down. Davis's shots took the shooter in the neck and under the jaw, folding him in a heap like dirty laundry. Bolan's ears were ringing, but he nodded once in acknowledgment to Davis nonetheless. The kid was good.

Bolan urged the Dodge back toward the Detroit police, who were using their vehicles as cover and firing straggler shots into what little resistance remained. As quickly as it had begun, the worst of it seemed to be over. Bolan hit the brakes suddenly, jerking the car to a stop, and leaned out his window, tagging a running gunman who was trying to break for a nearby alleyway. The man went down yelling, with a bullet in his leg, and Bolan was out of the rolling car with his Beretta in his fist.

Behind him, Davis scrambled into the driver's seat and stepped on the brake again before shifting the battle-torn Dodge into Park.

Bolan was on his quarry like a hawk on a mouse. The shooter rolled onto his back, his leg spraying blood from a bad wound, his face already pale as he brought up his TEC-9. The Executioner slapped the ungainly weapon aside as he landed on the wounded man's chest with one knee, driving the air out of the gunner's chest.

"Junk," Bolan said, snatching the TEC-9 from the man's hand. He shoved the black muzzle of the Beretta into his face. "Always were a jam waiting to happen."

"I want a lawyer!" the disarmed shooter squealed. "I got rights!"

"Give me a name," Bolan said. "Or all you'll get will be a bullet in the brain when I'm finished with you."

The dialogue sounded corny even to Bolan, but it was the kind of language spoken by punks-for-hire. Bolan could hear Davis coming up behind him and hoped the young detective wouldn't overreact to the soldier's bluff.

"A name," Bolan said. Sirens were erupting from the lot across the street as the police, having cleared their part of the gun battle, moved to seal off the area. It would be only moments before some of them blundered into this little scene. Bolan didn't have time for that. He heard Davis behind him, running interference as the first of the Detroit PD closed in and started asking questions. He gave Davis mental points for that. The kid was doing well during his trial by fire. The noise and activity behind them increased as emergency response personnel started to arrive. More Detroit PD were showing up by the carload, too. The sudden war on this already tainted city block had brought half the department out in a bid to clamp down on the chaos.

In the noise and confusion, it shouldn't have been a surprise that Bolan's prisoner tried to make play. The knife came out with surprising speed. Bolan heard the *snick* of the blade opening just as he caught the movement; he was ready for it. He grabbed the would-be killer's knife hand and wrist in a crushing grip. Behind him, Davis gasped, probably because he was watching Bolan's knuckles go white. Something cracked in the wounded man's hand and he yelped. The folding combat knife fell to the pavement.

"Give me a name," Bolan repeated. "Or I'll break the other one."

"Don't know," the man blurted, shaking his head as his pride gave way to pain. "Contract job. Never saw a face."

"Contract on who?" Bolan demanded.

"Jacket..." the man said, gritting his teeth. "Jacket pocket."

Bolan carefully reached into the man's jacket and pulled out a crumpled sheet of paper. The sheet was a photocopy of a photograph. The photograph showed Bolan meeting with Adam Davis outside the station house to which Davis was assigned. It was grainy and had obviously been taken with long-distance equipment. Bolan's face was circled in a whorl of yellow highlighter.

Bolan signaled to the police officers nearby, who closed in to take custody of the wounded shooter. The Executioner led the confused Davis several paces away from the main knot of uniforms and support personnel before showing him the paper.

"But this..." Davis looked at it. "What does it mean?"

"It means somebody knew to watch," Bolan said.

"Watch for what?"

"Outside interference." Bolan folded the paper and pocketed it. Turning, he watched the wounded gunman being ushered, under guard, to an ambulance that was just rolling up. Several men in suits, badges displayed prominently on their belts, clustered around Bolan and Davis, giving them the hairy eyeball; these would be Detroit detectives eager to ask this representative from Washington just what the hell was going on, and what Bolan thought he was doing. The soldier could almost write this dialogue himself; he had heard it often enough.

Bolan took out his secure smartphone and began moving deliberately from corpse to corpse, kneeling over his fallen enemies with the phone so he could snap their pictures. Davis followed him, looking as if he was ready to draw the Glock he had only just reholstered. Bolan couldn't blame the kid. The abrupt battle had the Executioner's own system working against the fight-or-flight dump of adrenaline that lingered even though the gunfight itself was over.

"What did you mean by 'outside interference,' Agent Cooper?" Davis spoke up.

"Somebody knows that a Justice Department agent was assigned to poke around this case," Bolan said. "Seeing you with me was all it took for our man with the telephoto lens, or whoever hired him, to finger me as that agent."

"You're talking about somebody inside the Department."

"I am," Bolan said.

"You don't sound surprised."

"I'm not." Bolan continued his grisly work, photographing all of the dead men. Then he walked to the bullet-riddled Charger and put his back to the car's pocked flank. "Keep an eye out for me while I do this," he said.

Davis nodded. He watched nervously, looking this way and that, hand near his gun, as Bolan transmitted the photographs and a terse report of what had produced them. The Farm would collect the data and run the images through advanced facial recognition software, comparing the dead men to profiles in meta-databases across the globe. There was no law enforcement or government agency whose files Stony Man Farm could not access. At least, if there was, it was hard even for Bolan to imagine what those might be.

No, if these men had criminal records, Barbara Price and her people would dig them up. Bolan had no doubt that most if not all of the shooters would have long rap sheets. Things would get really interesting, however, when Bolan had the chance to see just where these gunners' backgrounds pointed.

In the meantime, he would just have to keep shaking the tree, despite the target painted on his back. Davis, as his liaison, was no safer.

"You think I'm a dirty cop?" Davis asked bluntly. The steel in the man's tone was mildly surprising. Again Bolan raised his estimation of the younger man.

Bolan looked at Davis. "If I thought that, I wouldn't have asked you what I did."

Davis looked away. Bolan could see him thinking about it. Finally, the set of Davis's shoulders relaxed. "You're right," he said. "Everyone knows it, and nobody wants to say it out loud. Everyone knows the walls have ears. Nobody wants to say who's on the take and who isn't."

Bolan nodded. He didn't say so, but he liked that Davis was still idealistic enough to be offended when he thought his integrity was being challenged. There wasn't enough of that in the world, as far as Bolan was concerned.

"Is the CIA analyzing your pictures?" Davis ventured.

"Not exactly," Bolan said.

"But somebody is," Davis pressed. "You're running identifications on the gunmen."

"Which reminds me," Bolan said. "Make sure we get a full run-up on the guy they're taking in."

"I'll check back with the station and make sure. Unless someone suicides our boy in Holding."

Bolan looked at Davis sharply. The detective managed not to grin for only a moment.

Bolan shook his head. "Let's hope not." Davis laughed.

The pair surveyed the damage to the Dodge Charger, but it was clear the car was critically wounded. Bolan paused just long enough to grab the rental car agreement from the glove compartment and pocket it.

"I don't think you're going to get your security deposit back," Davis said mildly.

"I almost never do," Bolan said.

Davis managed to beg, borrow, or steal an unmarked Crown Victoria from among the police personnel on the scene. He did not explain and Bolan did not ask. The silver-gray sedan was among three other vehicles parked along the increasingly crowded, chaotic street.

Bolan climbed in as Davis brought up the car, transferring his war bag from the Dodge to the Ford. As he did so, Davis pointed past him to the cordon being set up. There were a pair of television vans and a crowd of reporters gathering, shouting questions at the officers keeping them at bay.

"That's going to be trouble, isn't it?" Davis said.

"Yeah," Bolan told him. "Nothing we can do about that now. Let's get started." He looked through the list Davis had provided and read the first address aloud. "You know this place?"

"There isn't a cop in the city who doesn't," Davis said. "It's not exactly one of our more affluent neighborhoods. A real hellhole, to be honest, Agent Cooper."

Bolan said nothing at first. He opened his war bag and removed several loaded 20-round magazines for the Beretta. Davis looked over, wide-eyed, as he caught a glimpse of the hardware and ordnance inside.

"You don't exactly travel light, do you, Agent Cooper?"

"If I could carry more, I would," Bolan said. He began replacing magazines in the pouches of his shoulder holster. "Welcome to the war, kid."

"Yeah," Davis said. "Yeah."

3

The squalid tenements on either side of the narrow street were crawling with people and sagging with furniture, garbage and other debris. A tangled maze of clotheslines linked facing buildings across the channel dividing them. As the unmarked Crown Victoria threaded its way around a series of abandoned, stripped vehicles, some of them bearing the scorch marks of past fires, children and adults scattered. Davis drove while Bolan watched from the passenger seat, his eyes scanning the rooftops and tracking the figures that ducked in and out of the shadows. The Executioner was no stranger to house-to-house close-quarters battle in urban environments. This neighborhood looked like yet another battleground awaiting the first shot to be fired.

"I hate coming down here," Davis said. "It's like a war zone sometimes."

Bolan nodded. He checked the list Davis had given him. "According to this," he said, "we want 1021, third floor, apartment C. A Ms. Kendall Brown. It looks like her son Mikyl was the first documented victim of these ritualized blade murders."

"Kendall Brown," Davis repeated. "Got it."

It took them a while to find the right building, as most

of the designations were either worn, missing completely, or covered by piles of junk or even cardboard signs. In a few cases, the numbers on the buildings had been spray-painted over or even switched. Bolan raised an eyebrow at one of the more obvious examples; the street signs at that intersection were also missing on one side.

"Trying to hide," Davis explained. "Could be a lot of things. Enemy gangs. Rival dealers. Creditors, tax collectors, any of countless state agencies, like Child Protective under the Department of Human Services. Most of the veteran agency folks know where they need to go, so these games don't fool anybody. But I bet it's hell trying to get a pizza delivered."

The dark humor in Davis's comment, which seemed otherwise unlike what Bolan had seen of the man so far, bespoke bitter experience, perhaps as a uniformed cop on the streets. Bolan let it go. He had seen enough ghettos and poverty-stricken crime zones like this one the world over to know it for what it was. It didn't matter if a place like this existed among the shantytowns of a third world banana republic, or in some of the worst overrun cesspools in Europe, or anywhere in the industrialized West. Poverty and desperation were feeding and breeding grounds for predators, who made those very problems worse, as they incestuously preyed on the communities that spawned them.

Bolan's jaw tightened. As many times as he saw this, it always moved something in him. There were innocents here, among the predators. They would be vulnerable to the creatures that hunted among them, terrorized them, bullied and brutalized and subjugated them. It turned the soldier's stomach.

Davis parked the car as close to the building as he could, wedging it between a derelict pickup truck—the rusted bed was full of trash—and a garbage bin overflowing with neglected refuse. The two men could hear children playing in the bin. When the detective leaned on the horn, the kids took the hint and climbed out, scampering off while shooting glares of mistrust and disappointment back at Bolan and Davis.

"One of them's going to get picked up and thrown into the back of a garbage truck one of these days," he said.

"No time soon, from the look of it." Bolan shook his head. "You'd better wait here."

"I was worried you were going to argue with me about that," Davis said. "I'll keep the motor running."

"Good idea." Bolan nodded. He reached into his war bag and removed a pair of translucent plastic cases. Inside each case was an earpiece that resembled a wireless telephone earbud. Bolan fitted one of the small devices behind his left ear, where it all but disappeared. He offered the second case to Davis.

"What's this?" Davis asked, accepting the earbud.

"These are short-range transceivers," Bolan said. "They're smart. They filter gunfire but provide good, audible communication between them. Speak in a normal tone of voice. You'll be able to listen in on everything I'm doing, and I'll be able to hear you if you speak or if anything goes down."

"Standard issue at the Justice Department, Agent Cooper?" Davis said. He tucked the earpiece in his own ear.

"Something like that," Bolan said. The devices had been developed, in fact, with the help of Stony Man Farm electronics genius Hermann "Gadgets" Schwarz. Bolan had used them in the field many times.

"The useful range varies," he told Davis. "If we get too far away to hear each other, there's a problem." He paused, double-checked and stowed his Beretta, and then checked the massive .44 Magnum Desert Eagle before replacing the handcannon in the Kydex holster behind his hip.

"Cooper," Davis said.

Bolan stopped with his hand on the door handle, shouldering his canvas war bag with his free arm. "Yeah?"

"You're not a cop." It was not a question.

"No," Bolan said. "I'm not."

"Look, Cooper," Davis said. "I *am* a cop, and I like to think I'm a good one. I know this place. It's very unlikely anybody's going to talk to you up there. You'll be lucky even to find this Brown woman at home, and if you do, she probably won't open the door for you. Nobody sees anything here, Cooper. They don't call the police if they can help it, which means if they do call, all hell is breaking loose down here. They don't talk to anybody if they don't have to. It's like this isn't even the United States down here, Cooper. It's bad. I know you're some kind of government superhero or something, but it could be that all you'll accomplish in there is burning the place down around your ears."

"Understood," Bolan said. "Keep your eyes open, Detective."

Davis nodded. He watched, looking anxious, as Bolan made his way through the scattered garbage at ground level to enter the tenement.

The smell hit Bolan as soon as he cleared the outer doorway. The stairwell reeked of refuse, human waste and mold. There was a mound of trash blocking the inner entrance; he stepped over it, hands ready to go for the Beretta under his jacket.

The floor was covered in carpet so stained its original color was impossible to determine. It creaked under Bolan's combat boots. Through the thin walls, he could hear and smell the usual signs of living at close quarters in an environment like this. Televisions blared. Repellant food odors hung heavy in the air. A domestic altercation of some kind simmered in one of the apartments he passed; there were angry screams in both Spanish and English. Bolan paused, hand drifting nearer the Beretta, wondering if intervention was required, until the voices grew more calm and quieted.

He moved on.

"Cooper," Davis's voice sounded in his ear. "Do you work alone?"

"What?" Bolan asked.

"There's an old blue Chevy Caprice full of guys down here," Davis said. "They've circled the block twice now, but I can't read the plate from where I'm watching. They're a little out of place in this neighborhood, and I don't recognize them. I was kind of hoping you were going to say you had called in reinforcements."

"No such luck," Bolan said. "Watch yourself down there, Davis. Keep me informed if anything changes."

"Will do."

Bolan picked up his pace. He traversed the next stairwells with less caution; he could feel the numbers working against him and Davis. When he reached the third floor, he found apartment C and stepped well to the side of the doorway. He flattened himself against the wall, reached out and rapped on the edge of the hollow-core door.

It took several tries before he got a response from within. Finally, a woman's voice answered, "What do you want?"

"Kendall Brown?" Bolan asked, as he came to the front of the door.

The door opened to the length of its chain revealing a middle-aged black woman wearing a T-shirt and sweatpants and bracing a toddler on her hip with one thick arm. The little girl, who was chewing on a pacifier, looked up at Bolan with wide eyes.

The woman nodded slowly. "What do you want?" she said again.

"I'm sorry to bother you, ma'am," he said, smiling briefly at the child. She continued to regard Bolan with amazement. "I need to talk to you about Mikyl Brown, your son."

The woman wanted to shut the door; Bolan could see her knuckles turn white. To her credit, she held her ground.

"Cooper," Davis said over their wireless connection. "I think that car I saw is parked behind the building. I saw it nose out and then reverse."

"Mikyl is dead," Brown said. "Murdered. Police already been here. Can't say they much cared about him, if you ask me. But they were here. They asked their questions. They left. Mikyl is still dead. What the hell you think you're gonna do now?"

"I understand," Bolan said. "I really do, Ms. Brown. I'm hoping that if I can better understand the circumstances of Mikyl's death, I can bring his killer to justice. I'm part of a special task force."

"Cooper," Davis's voice sounded in Bolan's ear again. "Cooper, I think you'd better hurry."

Kendall Brown closed the door, removed the chain and opened it again, after putting the child on the ground and giving the girl a gentle pat to send her toddling in the opposite direction. She lowered her voice. "I don't know who you are, mister," she said, "but it's damned cruel what you're doing. Mikyl was murdered in a gang fight. Stabbed to death. The boy who done it, not even a year older than my son, is in prison. Probably get out sooner than he should, too. Just how things go."

Bolan's eyes narrowed. "Mikyl's murderer was convicted?"

"Cooper." Davis's voice was growing more urgent.

"Who the hell are you, mister?" Brown said. "I don't need you coming up in here and reminding me of my boy." She slammed the door in his face with considerable force. Bolan looked up and down the corridor; nothing moved.

"I'm coming out," Bolan said. "Something's not right, here. Keep the front covered."

"Understood," Davis answered.

Bolan paused at the stairwell. Beneath the noise of the

apartments, both in and outside the building, he could hear something else.

Shuffling. There were men in the stairwell.

Bolan reached into the canvas war bag. He removed a flashbang grenade, popped the pin and watched the spoon spring free.

Below him, someone moved in response to the noise.

The soldier leaned over the stairwell railing and let the grenade fall.

He turned away, shielding his ears with his palms, squeezing his eyes shut. The actinic flash of the grenade was bright enough that he could see it through his eyelids. The thunderclap of the less-lethal bomb made his teeth vibrate. He heard a scream.

No sooner had the flash faded than Bolan hoisted himself up over the railing. He dropped, colliding heavily on the landing below, absorbing the impact with his legs. Rising from his crouch, he drew the double-edged combat-survival dagger in his waistband. The trio of men in whose midst he had landed, either held or were reaching for automatic weapons. They were dressed in what Bolan recognized as expensive suits, probably tailored to hide their shoulder holsters and submachine-gun harnesses. All three continued rubbing at their eyes or holding their ears.

The nearest of the gunmen managed to fix Bolan with bloodshot eyes, fighting the involuntary tears streaming down his face. His gun came up, but Bolan stabbed him in the neck and ripped the knife forward and away. The dying man spun, spraying the wall crimson.

Bolan kicked out the knee of the second man, dropping him to the floor. The third was on his hands and knees, trying to find the micro-Uzi he had dropped. The Executioner fired a kick to his ribs and was rewarded with an audible crack as the gunman rolled over. He threw his knife arm backward, sensing the second man surging back to his feet, and rammed the double-edged blade into the hollow of the gunner's throat. Yanking the knife out in a circular motion as he wrenched the man's head around, the soldier levered him down to die on the stairs.

Bolan checked left, right, and then up and down the stairwell, very quickly. Then he threw himself to the floor, landing with his knee in the back of the man he had rib-kicked. Air gasped from the gunman's lungs and he lost his grip on the Uzi again. Bolan kicked the gun away and moved to secure the man; he had plastic zip-tie cuffs in his pocket. He rolled his prisoner over so the man's back was on the floor.

The would-be killer wasn't down for the count. His hand snaked into his jacket and came out with a backup pistol, a tiny chromed .25ACP. He fired a single round. Bolan swatted the gun aside and plunged the blade of his knife into the most quickly lethal target. The blade penetrated the gunner's eye and turned him off as if a switch had been thrown.

Bolan drew a breath.

He followed the path of the bullet, but it had lodged in the railing of the stairwell, taking chips from the paint. The small-caliber slug would not have been much of a threat, but the whole point of Bolan's maneuver had been to neutralize these attackers before they started firing at close quarters. Most pistol and machine-gun rounds would pass right through an interior wall of a dwelling. They would penetrate most exterior walls, for that matter. In slums like these, gunfire would scythe through the residents as if the walls weren't there. Bolan could not permit that to happen, which meant he had to keep moving, and quickly, to get clear of the tenement.

"Davis," Bolan said quietly, wiping his knife clean on one of the dead men's jackets. He sheathed the blade. "I have engaged multiple hostiles. Well dressed and heavily armed." He began methodically stripping the gunmen's weapons, separating slides and bolts from receivers and tossing the results in opposite directions. "See if you can get some uniforms in here, including the medical examiner. Tell them to sweep the building," he suggested. "I don't want to leave a lot of fire-arms in component parts for the neighborhood kids to play with." He took a moment to snap pictures of the dead men and transmit them to Stony Man Farm.

Bolan took the stairs two and three at a time as he made his way back down, counting on speed and initiative to save him should there be any more shooters positioned as backup somewhere below. When he hit ground level, he made his way for the rear of the building, stepping over a homeless man sleeping in the alcove. The street person shouted curses after the soldier, who ignored them.

Bolan spotted the gunman's car, parked exactly where Davis said it would be. There were two thugs sitting in it, one on the passenger side and one behind the wheel.

Bolan drew the Beretta 93-R and flicked the selector switch to 3-round burst.

They noticed him coming before he got more than a few steps. Bolan saw the driver bring a small handheld two-way radio to his face. He was lining up the men in the car for a shot when the first bullet hit the pavement at his feet.

There were more gunmen, hidden behind the building—a lot more. There had to be at least one other vehicle Davis hadn't seen. The gunmen were grouped on the fire escape of the adjacent position, covering the rear entrance from eleva-tion. No doubt they thought this afforded them the tactical advantage.

Against any man but the Executioner, it would have.

Bolan rolled into a tight ball and threw himself forward and right, behind the concrete abutment supporting the metal posts of the roof over the rear entrance. Bullets kicked up cement dust as automatic gunfire ripped through the space between the tenements. Beyond that, Bolan could hear the shouts of men and women reacting to the sudden warfare in their midst. In a neighborhood as bad as this, they would be accustomed to the occasional shot, even a short exchange among gangs or rival drug dealers. A prolonged firefight like this would be something else entirely, and cause for real concern among even the most hardened denizens of this Detroit ghetto.

Bolan was pinned down. He could not retreat through the building at his back; that would invite the gunmen into the tenement, too, which was the problem he had just worked to avoid. He could not break right or left; that would give the shooters a clear shot. They would pick him off easily before he got the chance to shoot them all.

His only way out was directly across the alley, into the space beneath the shooters, where the fire escape itself would foul their aim. He braced himself, coiling his body like a spring, and prepared to make a dash for it.

Breaking for it, Bolan threw himself into the alleyway.

The parked car wasn't parked anymore. It was moving at speed—and coming right for him.

4

The Crown Victoria barreled down the narrow alleyway from the opposite direction. The gunmen in the Chevy saw it coming and tried to swerve, only to sheer bricks from the tenement on the driver's side. Davis pushed the car's engine to the red line. The vehicles collided with a scream of metal on metal and roaring 8-cylinder power plants. With his foot apparently still pushed all the way to the floor, Davis leaned out of his open window, extended his Glock and pumped its entire magazine into the windshield of the gunmen's car.

Bolan couldn't afford to admire Davis's handiwork. The shooters on the fire escape did their best to track him and gun him down, but he was moving too fast, his rush under their guns had been just unexpected enough to work. When he was directly below them, he flattened himself against the building, raised the Beretta skyward in a two-handed grip and started firing.

To the men on the fire escape, the world erupted in flying, burning metal. Bolan's rounds punched through from below, ricocheting from the metal grates of the upper landing, turning the metal basket in which they stood into a blood-soaked nightmare. One of the men above managed to trigger a blast that went wide, digging a furrow near Bolan's heels, before he went down.

Footsteps sounded at one end of the alley mouth.

"Cooper!" Davis yelled as he reloaded his Glock. "More coming!"

Bolan ran for the passenger side of the car, ripped open the door and jumped in, pulling the door shut against damaged hinges. Davis slammed the gearshift into Reverse and stepped on it, sending the car skidding back the way it had come.

"Where to?" Davis asked.

"Get us back onto the street," Bolan said, reloading the Beretta. He racked the slide. "You know this area. Where can we go where there are fewer people?"

"Two blocks over," Davis said without hesitation. "There's a strip of old commercial and residential structures targeted for urban renewal. Most of it's boarded up. There are some homeless camped there, but not too many during the day. It's more or less deserted right now."

"Perfect. Don't spare the gas."

Davis pushed them through sparse traffic. A vehicle appeared to be following them—Bolan assumed it was the car Davis hadn't seen, the one that had to have been nearby to transport the assassins—and where there was one, there might be more. Despite Davis's skilled driving, the pursuit car began to gain on them.

Bolan drew the Desert Eagle from its Kydex holster.

"How did they find us?" Davis asked.

"They had to know where we would be," Bolan said.

"Somebody in the department," Davis said, frowning. "Somebody with access to my files. The list of addresses."

Bolan said nothing for a moment. He was watching the hostiles' car come up on their passenger-side flank. "Give us a burst of speed and then put us into a side street," he said. "Get ready to bail out. Follow my lead."

"Right," Davis said.

The chase car drew alongside their vehicle, and the Executioner was waiting. The armed men inside the car, dressed in cheap suits like they were refugees from a business meeting, began to shift into place, going for weapons held below the level of their windows.

Bolan rolled down his own window and thrust the triangular snout of the Desert Eagle into the wind. He triggered a single shot. The .44 Magnum hollowpoint round blew apart the driver's-side front tire.

Davis was no slouch behind the wheel. He jammed on the brakes and pulled the steering wheel hard to the right, ramming the nose of their vehicle into the rear flank of the chase car. The gunmen spun out, the maneuver that much more violent thanks to the wreckage of the front tire. Spikes flew in a tight arc as the rim cut through what was left of the steel-belted radial.

Davis continued his push and shot past the rear end of the chase car. He cut over again, pacing the front of the row of boarded buildings, until he found an enclosure that might have been a carport or an abandoned loading dock. Plywood splintered and flew apart as the grille of the Crown Victoria rammed past makeshift barriers.

"Out, out, out," Bolan ordered. Davis bailed out of the car with him. Bolan pointed. "Take the back. I'll take the front." The other side of the narrow, crumbling city block was only a few sheets of plywood or molding drywall away; if Davis could not find an exit ready-made on the other side, he could easily make one. Bolan drew the Beretta 93-R left-handed and, with a weapon in each hand, headed for the ragged, gaping hole the car had made with its passing.

An almost eerie sense of déjà vu hit him as his enemies converged. The gunmen, looking for all the world like stereotypical mafiosi, were armed with a mismatched assortment of handguns, shotguns and automatic small arms. They were coming around both sides of the crippled chase car when one of them spotted Bolan emerging from the carport.

The soldier was a combat shooter borne of both training and long experience. He knew the mistakes men made in armed battle, and he knew how to exploit these mistakes. In a half crouch, walking smoothly and quickly with a gliding, heel-to-toe gait, he came at them, his weapons extended, his wrists canted at very slight angles to bolster the stability of each shooting wrist and maximize the visibility of his sights. The Executioner bore down on them, irresistible force and immovable object in one battle-ready vessel.

He fired.

The Desert Eagle bucked in his fist, its gas-operated action, tuned by Stony Man Farm armorer John "Cowboy" Kissinger, cycling smoothly and lethally in Bolan's grip. The Beretta sang in deadly harmony, tapping out a staccato rhythm with each squeeze of the trigger. Bolan's 3-shot bursts found their mark, stitching first one, then another, blasting the gunmen center of mass. The Desert Eagle's heavier rounds took two more targets as Bolan angled for precise head shots. The hollowpoint slugs dug wide holes through their targets. Bolan's mercy, for mercy it was, lay in a quick end to enemy lives lived cruelly and violently.

Bolan never stopped moving, never stopped closing in. As he got to contact distance he fired a triburst through the throat of one man, emptying the Beretta's 20-round magazine. He fired the last shot in the Desert Eagle, too, but that did not slow him. Instead he savagely pistol-whipped the nearest gunman, bringing the butt of the Desert Eagle down across the bridge of the man's nose. He drove a follow-up knee strike into the man's abdomen and then slammed the empty pistol onto the back of the man's neck as the gunman doubled over.

His foes were all neutralized.

Still moving, seeking cover behind the chase car, he reloaded and checked every direction around him. Rarely was a professional killed by the enemy he could see; the deadliest bullets came from guns fired by unseen hands. Bolan, once in combat, maintained vigilant awareness of his battlefield throughout the engagement.

He heard the steady cracks of Davis's Glock from the other side of the abandoned structure he faced. The pistol's bark was punctuated by long, withering blasts from an automatic weapon. It was a Kalashnikov rifle, judging from the distinctly hollow metallic sound Bolan knew only too well. Davis was outgunned, for certain—but not for long.

Bolan holstered the Beretta and held the Desert Eagle before him in a two-handed grip. He ran for the gap separating two almost contiguous buildings, turning sideways and pushing the weapon forward in his right as he sidestepped. He cleared the far side, looking for Davis—

A tire iron missed his head by inches.

The soldier's habitual combat half-crouch saved him. The enemy, a middle-aged man in a three-piece suit whose head was as bald as an egg, swung the tire iron again, trying to bring it down on his adversary's shoulder, perhaps to break his clavicle. Bolan snapped out a low side kick and broke the man's ankle.

There was a revolver in the thug's belt, but Bolan took quick note of the long, empty casings on the ground. They were .357 Magnum shells, at a glance. Bolan and his attacker stood in the lee of an abandoned, burned-out station wagon that had to be more than thirty-years-old. Beyond that, Davis, taking shelter behind a makeshift battlement consisting of a stack of rusted and stripped appliances dumped in front of the building, was holding his own. He was firing from cover at a knot of gunmen crouched behind a concrete barrier. The barrier was apparently something installed to prevent through traffic.

The bald man was howling in pain. He clutched at his

ankle and made no attempt to go for the gun in his belt. Bolan surmised that this was why he'd been wielding a tire iron in the first place. Evidently he had run out of ammunition and had withdrawn to a backup position, perhaps even lying in wait for Bolan specifically. If that was true, and odds were good that it was, the opposition was even more organized than the soldier had suspected. This implied not just professional, paid hitters, but gunners of at least moderate experience.

Bolan paused long enough to secure the injured man with two sets of plastic zip-tie cuffs, binding the prisoner's hands and then securing his good leg to his wrists. That would hold him for the moment, anyway; there was no time to do more.

The Executioner took a two-handed grip on the Desert Eagle and braced himself against the roof of the derelict station wagon. As he did so, one of the gunners tracking Davis saw him and jumped up. He swung his Kalashnikov in a wide arc, trying to track Bolan while holding the trigger down and spraying on full-auto.

The bullets went wide. The shots ripped across the torso of the fallen hitter, ripping open his chest and killing him. Bolan took careful aim and put a single .44 Magnum slug through the left eye of the man who had done it. The gunman fell instantly, firing out the remainder of his magazine harmlessly into the littered asphalt. Bolan ducked briefly to avoid a bees' nest of ricochets.

He fired once, then again. Twice his bullets found their marks, snapping back the skulls of gunmen who did not realize they were vulnerable. The distance was long for a pistol, but there was no finer long-distance marksman than Bolan. The soldier waited to see if another enemy would be careless enough to move into the kill zone. There was more gunfire from the opposite side of the barrier, which drove Davis back to cover as he tried to join in the fray.

The angle was bad. Bolan shifted his position to the other

end of the station wagon, but this presented a new problem. Davis was between him and the rest of the shooters.

Bolan carefully surveyed the situation. He watched for a rhythm, if any, as the gunmen broke cover to shoot at Davis and in Bolan's general direction. A few bullets struck the old station wagon. They were nowhere near him.

He spoke aloud for the benefit of his earbud transceiver.

"Davis," he said. "Duck."

The detective dropped immediately. Bolan fired once, taking one of the remaining gunmen between the eyes. The others reacted to that, crouching down more carefully behind their concrete shield. Bolan simply waited.

Somewhere in the distance, police sirens could be heard. The firefight had finally drawn the attention of law enforcement. Davis hadn't had a chance to call for backup, at least not while within the range that Bolan could overhear. No doubt the gunfire itself had generated frantic calls from citizens near this abandoned zone.

"Stay down," Bolan said.

Bolan retrieved a fragmentation grenade from his war bag. He pulled the pin, let the spoon pop free and waited, counting in his head. Davis caught the movement and eyed him curiously from his vantage point, covering the top of his head with his folded arms as he lay on his stomach. Bolan nodded once and then tossed the grenade.

The bomb exploded just as it hit the lip of the concrete barrier. The men not caught by shrapnel from the grenade absorbed the spray of concrete fragments the explosion kicked up. Guns clattered to the pavement. As the boom echoed from the nearby brick buildings, nothing else moved.

Davis pushed himself to his feet.

Bolan moved from cover. He walked over, weapon ready, listening and watching to see if another ambush would be forthcoming. They had been attacked too many times already for him not to expect it at any moment. The sirens continued to close, but they were still some distance off.

"They're going to take a few minutes to find us," Davis said.

"Do I look that excited?" Bolan asked.

"You're a one-man war, Cooper," Davis said. "And I'm willing to bet this won't be the first time you catch hell for walking into someone's jurisdiction and setting the place on fire."

"You catch on fast, Detective," Bolan said. In his pocket, his secure satellite phone began to vibrate. He snapped it open.

"Cooper," he said. Using his cover identity would inform the Farm that there were others present.

"Striker," Barbara Price said. "I hear police."

"Yeah," Bolan said. "You do. I've just engaged targets comprising a hit team. Armed professionals, mixed kit. Civilian clothing on the formal side. You caught me before I could send you pictures. I'd actually like to take those before company gets here."

"Do so," the Farm's mission controller told him. "We have a database pulled up. I'll explain when you're ready."

Bolan made a fast circuit of the dead men closest to him and Davis. The ones on the other side of the abandoned building would have to wait. He said as much to Price when he reestablished the connection.

"You may not need to," Price said. "We're working on a theory, and Bear has some preliminary, rough matches pulled up. It looks like we're right." Aaron "the Bear" Kurtzman was Stony Man Farm's resident computer genius.

"Why?" Bolan said. "What's the theory?"

"Your gunmen," Price told him, "are old school Mafia. Hit men for the Mob."

Bolan took that in for a moment. He had, over the course of his war, been on the receiving end of Mob guns before, even had a price on his head. It was among the Mafia that the Executioner had first become known, then famous, then infamous.

"I thought something seemed familiar about all this," he said, deadpan.

He could sense the smile in Price's voice. "I'll bet," she said. She went on more seriously. "We've checked the pictures you sent first, and checked them thoroughly. Each one of those men has a rap sheet. Most of them are career criminals. A few are young enough that they haven't quite reached the majors, but they were headed that way before you got to them. Each and every one has ties, directly or indirectly, to Detroit-area underworld figures."

Davis, unable to hear Price's side of the conversation, shot Bolan a quizzical look.

"But that doesn't scan at all," Bolan said, considering her report. "Unless..."

"Unless your cover has been breached and the whole of the Michigan Mafia wants your head?" Price said. "We thought of that. Your cover is secure. There's been no chatter from the usual sources that we would see if word about you got out. There's no reason to believe anyone's targeting you for any reason other than the obvious—you're an interloping federal agent looking into these serial killings."

"Something's not right where that's concerned, either," Bolan said. "But I need to see where that takes me before I offer any theories of my own. So why would Detroit's Mob be involved?"

"The most obvious reason is that they're the prime employee pool for a job like this."

"Guns for hire," Bolan supplied. "You need a hit man or a lot of them in Detroit, a city notorious for its corruption, then you go see the Mob. Something like that?"

"Exactly," Price said. "Somebody with serious money, a

lot of clout, or both is behind this. Somebody with enough resources to throw that many Mafia gunners at one man."

"Or two," Bolan said, looking at Davis, who continued to watch him curiously.

"There's one good thing about all this," Price said.

"And that is?"

"You've made a serious dent in the local crime syndicates," Price said. "We'll continue to work up the other identifications you sent. I'll let you know if anything pops up."

"I'll stay after it on this end," Bolan said.

"Striker?" Price said. "Be careful. And good hunting."

"Thanks," Bolan said. "Cooper out." The sirens of the approaching police cars had become louder. Cruisers were pulling up around the abandoned buildings and closing on both sides. Bolan frowned. He shut his phone and looked at Davis. "Our boys—" he jerked his head at the dead men "—were all Mafia hit men. Hired to kill me, or to kill both of us."

"Cooper," Davis said, his face lurid in the red and blue lights of the approaching cruisers, "what's really going on here?"

"Murder, and covering up murder. It isn't the *what* that concerns me most," Bolan said. "It's the *who*."

5

Reginald Chamblis worked the blades through the air, feeling them move, feeling them *sing,* feeling them speak to him. Each was a custom bowie knife the exact length of his forearm. Each was razor sharp and handmade. As the cutting edges cleaved the air, as the needle tips of the blades thrust here and there, in and out, he saw the targets he was striking on a succession of phantom opponents.

He moved as he worked. The man was light on the balls of his feet, his knees slightly bent, his entire body coiled with dynamic tension. He stalked his way from one end of the training hall to other, the polished hardwood floor silent beneath him. In the corners, wooden kung fu dummies stood at mute attention, the sticks of their "arms" pointing at specified angles and heights. The rankings and awards arranged neatly on the far wall lent the place an air of respectability.

Not one of the certificates was less than ten years old.

Chamblis had spent his life working to find new and greater challenges. In high school, everything had come easily to him. He was well-liked, good-looking, athletic and smart. He excelled in his classes. He played football and basketball, though not quite at the level of those who earned scholarships for doing just that. He majored in business and minored, simply because he enjoyed it, in philosophy. He graduated with a 4.0 GPA and spent three of his four years at university as the editor of the school newspaper and president of half a dozen student organizations. He conquered it all— and at least a dozen of the campus's most desirable young women—and never appeared taxed in the slightest by any of it.

The truth was that even then, Chamblis was bored. He had never told anyone, but back in those days, he looked at the people around him who struggled to accomplish their goals and felt a mixture of envy and confusion. They confused him, because he did not understand how any human being could fail to achieve what he or she desired. He envied them, because he had come to associate his boredom with never being forced to work hard.

He vowed to change that.

He hit the street running after graduation. He parlayed his business degree into entry-level positions at first a finance firm, then a high-tech start-up. He moved to Detroit because, of all the cities he had ever visited, it was in Detroit that he had felt the least comfortable, the least safe. He set out to build a career there.

He currently owned three companies, all of them profitable, all of them controlled by him. His firms made circuit boards, time and frequency synchronization equipment, industrial toolholders and tool bits. He had been profiled in every major business magazine on both coasts; he was heralded as the man almost single-handedly bringing domestic manufacturing back to the United States.

It was in Detroit that he first thought to punish and challenge his body as well as his mind. He began studying martial arts. He earned a black belt, and then another. He moved from style to style, learning, doing, being, *becoming*.

And he was still bored.

He was rich. He could afford to hire other executives with

similar promise and drive to run his companies for him, and he did. He took up the sports of the idle rich, traveling the country and beyond. He found extreme sports, and for the briefest of moments, the adrenaline rush of cliff diving, of free climbing, of white-water rafting and other dangerous pursuits almost kept him interested. But it wasn't enough.

In his pursuit of that elusive adrenaline rush, that excitement that made life worth living, he met other men and even a few women who seemed to suffer similarly. He cultivated those friendships, using the charm that came so naturally to him. He weeded out those with limitations from those without. He surrounded himself with a knot of like-minded individuals. Together they strived to find the most dangerous of pastimes, the most daring of sporting pursuits.

It wasn't enough. Then, everything changed.

The martial artist in him drove him to pursue various weapons arts. He sought out specialty instructors across the country, paying them exorbitant sums for their private, undivided attention. He went on group trips, too. One such trip in the Midwest offered dangerous free climbing to a remote cliff-top location, followed by a weekend of training in knife fighting. After that first weekend, Chamblis knew he was hooked. It was possible he had found a pursuit just lethal enough, just deadly enough or potentially so, that studying it could hold his interest.

Life was not done changing for him, however.

Chamblis was walking to his parked car after leaving the airport. He had just finished his second annual attendance of the knife fighting weekend that had so enthralled him. He was carrying, in a heavy, padded case, the custom-made knives crafted for him by a local knife maker. He had used the knives for his training. They were made to specifications for him and him alone.

The two vagrants came at him from the shadows. He smelled them before he heard them; they reeked of neglect, cheap alcohol and marijuana. The Detroit area had no short-age of marginalized street people like these. They were a product of bad economies as much as bad choices, human flotsam that collected in large cities as surely as leaves col-lected in a pool filter. At a glance, Chamblis knew these men were, individually, no match for him. They were in ill health, their skeletal forms racked by drugs, disease and years of ill use. One on one, he knew a hundred different ways to take out either of them. He could choose to neutralize them, to cripple them, to kill them.

They produced screwdrivers, and Chamblis knew sud-denly that it was not that simple. One man with a knife he could disarm using his training. Two men...that was a much riskier proposition. He was carrying weapons of his own under his arm. He quickly flipped open the case, snatching the knives out as the case itself hit the pavement.

The two attackers paused, but only for a moment. The haze numbing their minds to the distress of their bodies dulled their reaction time as well as their good sense. They came at him, their makeshift weapons poised to strike.

Chamblis let his training take over. He executed the forms, the techniques, the movements he had been taught. Fascinat-ing theory became bloody execution. He did it for the simple fact that it excited him to find out if he could. He was not disappointed.

He used his knives to kill both men. Not knowing what else to do, but believing firmly in the right of a rich man to kill two poor men with complete and utter impunity, he simply went home. He cleaned both blades and went to bed.

It was the best night's sleep of his life.

The next day, he found himself reliving that duel in his mind, over and over again. He could not get it out of his head. He reviewed every vivid detail, seared into his memory as it was. It was only that evening that he thought to check the news.

The television news did not bother to run the story. He found a small blurb buried in the newspaper the next morning. Two homeless men were believed to have stabbed each other to death. Chamblis knew better than anyone that the wounds were not consistent with the screwdrivers the homeless assailants had been carrying, but obviously few felt the need to delve too deeply into this nice, neat explanation for the deaths of two marginalized and powerless human beings.

Even as he thought those words he realized what they meant. Power over the powerless. The deaths of marginalized human beings. A "crime" that was as exhilarating as it was beneficial to everyone involved.

He admired his form in the full-length mirrors set against one wall of the studio. He commenced another complicated series of movements based on a Japanese kata from one of his more traditional martial arts. If his long-ago teachers could only see him. He smiled at the thought even as he exulted in the power his knives brought him.

He was finally excited. He was finally interested. In dueling, in pitting his life against others, in taking the oppositional human interaction to its most grave of intensities, he had found the means through which he could truly discover himself. Wisdom through mortal combat. Enlightenment through lethal play. It was his religion. It was his black magic. It was his reason for being.

Reginald Chamblis was a duelist, and he had always longed to be, even before he understood that call.

Over the next years Chamblis assembled a sporting club, of sorts, of like-minded individuals. It was extraordinarily hard to do this, especially at first, for there was no room for error. Approach even one man or woman who did not understand the beauty of the blade, who did not covet the revelatory power of using it on a human being in mortal, mutual combat, and he risked exposure. To be brought up on charges would ruin him. He could not allow that to happen, even if, through his money and his power, he managed to avoid conviction or prison time.

His connections in Detroit's halls of power helped. He was not perfect and he knew he would not be. In the years he spent assembling the membership of his dueling congress, he twice selected individuals whom he thought were ready, willing and capable of taking up the blade for real. Each one was a knife aficionado of great enthusiasm; each one had expressed little regard for the weak, for the helpless, for those who stood in the way of the individual's path to greatness. But each man, at the critical moment, turned coward and threatened to run to the police.

Chamblis had of course had both men killed. That was easily enough covered up, given who he knew and what he knew about those powerful local figures. But each time his failure was a sobering reminder of the gravitas of his chosen pursuit. He made sure that the other members of his club understood that and were party to the removal of these unworthy prospective members, even if after the fact. He was proud of his men and women of the knife; he would live and die for them, and they for him.

All save for one. The thought enraged him—

The phone rang. Already the drift in his thoughts was taking Chamblis out of the Zen mind of no mind, the state of awareness and being in the present, undistracted and focused, that was so critical to the lethal use of the blade against another human being so armed. He surrendered to the interruption, choking off a curse in his throat, and picked up the wireless smartphone that sat near the doorway on the hardwood floor. He snatched it up from where it rested next to his gym bag, placing his knives gently on the bag as he did so.

"Yes," he said, spitting the word.

"It's me," the familiar voice said. "Uh… It ain't good."

"*What* isn't good?" Chamblis demanded.

"Davis and his Justice Department goon are still alive,"

the voice answered. "The boys you hired are all…well, all done."

"What?"

"They're dead," the voice said. "This Cooper, he about started a war. There are bodies everywhere. My lieutenant is freaking out. There've been phone calls back and forth between us and the Feds for the last two hours. It's fucking *ugly,* man."

"Where are they now?"

"I don't know, man. Doing their thing, I guess."

"Find out!" Chamblis ordered. "Or else I'll make sure everybody you care about knows you're on the take before you wake up with your throat cut!"

"Hey, hey, let's not get out of control here," the voice wheedled. "It's cool, man. I'll take steps. It's just, you, well. You might wanna do the same, you know?"

"I'll take it under advisement," Chamblis said, disgusted. He hung up.

He paused to take several deep breaths. This was not the time to lose control. No, that would not do. He needed to focus, and he needed to solve this problem.

At least, he thought as he dialed the next number from memory, he wasn't bored. That was always something.

"Yes, Maestro." The voice of Andreas Garter was respectful, as always. Garter was his senior student and the man Chamblis trusted most.

"I need to know if you've found him," Chamblis said.

"No, Maestro." Garter sounded crestfallen. "Not yet. I can try calling him—"

"Don't you think I've tried that?" Chamblis demanded. "He does not answer."

"Forgive me, Maestro."

"No, no, it isn't you, Andreas," Chamblis said. "It's just… if Patrick goes on the way he's been, he risks exposing us all. It is imperative we stop him."

"Yes, Maestro."

"We have another problem. The men we hired failed."

"Maestro?" Garter sounded confused. "How can this be? There were so many, so well paid, so armed—"

"Nonetheless," Chamblis said, "it was not enough. I need you to make some more calls. Use the contacts I gave you previously. We require more men. Make sure the…contractors understand the gravity of the situation and are willing to do whatever is necessary. Reassure them that I will protect them if their masters cannot. It is within my power. But do not use my name unnecessarily, or with underlings."

"Of course not, Maestro. I would sooner die."

"I know, Andreas," Chamblis said. "I know. Make sure our people redouble their efforts. If we cannot find Patrick ourselves, we shall have to devise another way. Every moment he is on the streets is another moment he endangers us."

"I understand, Maestro."

Chamblis hung up. He put the phone down, took up his knives once more and threw himself into a furious set of movements that sent him leaping, ducking, diving, slashing and thrusting across the hall. The exertion helped clear his mind. As always, the purity of the blade, the knowledge of the knife, was everything. By the blade would his people be protected. By the blade would the scourge that was Patrick Farnham be eliminated.

The name, which came to him unbidden, soured his mood still further. If the prospective members he had been forced to kill were failures, Farnham was something else, some higher order of mistake. Farnham had been a full-fledged member of Chamblis's fellowship. He had dined in Chamblis's home, had been trusted with his inner thoughts. He had been as much friend as brother to Chamblis, as any other member of the club was. More so, in fact, for in Farnham, Chamblis had seen some part of himself, some common thread.

Farnham had lost his way, first gradually, then with alarming speed. It began as an air of secrecy that began to make the other members of Chamblis's fellowship feel as if their brother were mocking them. It was as if Farnham knew something they did not. Then, one day, Farnham had, perhaps believing Chamblis would see the wisdom in his words and actions, revealed everything.

He had stopped killing those society would not miss. He no longer confined his dueling practice to those within the club or those who would be killed quietly, discreetly. No, Farnham believed that for his dueling to have meaning, it had to come at any time, in any place, and that no man or woman could believe himself or herself safe from the blade. Farnham saw himself as judge and jury—no, as predator among prey. He was killing *mundanes*—ordinary men and women, random members of society—with joyous abandon. He boasted of choosing his targets arbitrarily, giving them knives with which to defend themselves before taking them apart with all the considerable skill he possessed. Of Farnham's skill, Chamblis had no doubt, for it was he who had trained the man.

But Farnham's indiscretions were bringing too much publicity. It was bad enough that Chamblis was forced to arrange for the removal of a police officer—which strained his relationship among the local police he paid so generously—and an agent of the federal government. But Chamblis knew as well as anyone that the media were going to break the story. A lot of pressure had been brought to bear, both locally and externally, to prevent that from happening. Chamblis did not pretend to understand the external pressure, although it hinted ominously at further government involvement. He had been glad to have whatever roadblocks could be erected to the publication of these "serial killings."

The fact that Farnham's work was thought to be the work of a serial killer galled him. The fellowship of the blade was supposed to be so much more than random murder. Chamblis did not know with whom to be more angry. He could hate the popular press for turning everything into a sensationalist and tasteless showmanship, or he could hate Farnham for debasing the blade by using it on those it was never meant to be used against.

To kill those on the fringes of society was a public service. To kill at random, simply to kill, there was no honor in that. There was no enlightenment in that. Farnham should understand that. The fact that he did not hurt Chamblis very much, for Farnham, as his student, was his responsibility.

He increased the intensity of his workout. Sweat began to pour from his face, from his bare arms in the sleeveless workout shirt he wore. His bare feet grabbed the hardwood. He moved with purpose. He let his range express itself in the movement of the knives. When he eviscerated his phantom enemy, he saw not some faceless invisible enemy, but Patrick Farnham.

Chamblis would eliminate the threats arrayed against him. The key to doing so was to eliminate the force that was creating so much undesired attention. Patrick Farnham was the problem. Eliminating Patrick Farnham was the solution.

Reginald Chamblis had created the mad dog that was Farnham.

It was Chamblis who would put down that rabid animal.

6

The door, which had been opened perhaps two inches, slammed shut in Davis's face. The young detective turned to Bolan in frustration. "I knew this was a difficult area to work," he said. "I didn't think we'd come up against a complete cold shoulder."

Bolan let him talk. He was pressed against the wall on the opposite side of the door, farther away than Davis, listening to the shuffling inside. He did not like what he was hearing. He pointed to the young detective and waved him away, urging him silently to move farther from the perimeter of the doorway. Davis looked confused, then alarmed, moving back and putting his hand on the butt of his gun.

After the hellscape that was their last foray into a residential neighborhood, it had been a near miss escaping the custody of the Detroit police. Davis's lieutenant, Johnson Sumner, had been almost apoplectic, ready to pull Davis off liaison duty and perhaps even place him in protective custody. It had taken the intervention of Brognola to smooth things over. The big Fed and the Justice Department had danced this dance countless times whenever the Executioner did what he did best in domestic target zones.

Whatever Brognola and the rest of his people at Justice

had said to the locals, it had immediately quashed any talk of taking Bolan and Davis into custody. The detective had been tersely ordered to continue in his role as liaison, despite Lieutenant Sumner's grousing about the body count. Though he was the primary cause behind that mounting figure, Bolan was not unsympathetic. The lieutenant was just trying to do his job and keep the peace. No man liked to see a flamethrower taken to his barn, even if the fire drove out the rats.

This location was the fourth they had visited so far. Each was in similarly decrepit circumstances, although the addresses ranged around the city. The fact was that Detroit had no shortage of bad neighborhoods. It had been that way for as long as Bolan could remember, for he was no stranger to the city.

Nevertheless, he felt as if he were getting a guided tour through some of the city's more dangerous areas. To Bolan, this was like a fisherman touring rich seas, and the predators plaguing Detroit were the prey with which Bolan was so intimately familiar.

The first location housed a family who had, in fact, lost a loved one to a tragic stabbing. It had taken only a little bit of questioning to determine that this crime, too, had been solved. The circumstances bore no similarity to the modus operandi of the serial stabbings currently vexing the Detroit authorities. The family still grieved its loss. They were cooperative, but angry nonetheless. They did not appreciate having bad memories unearthed.

The second location was a complete bust. The address was a vacant house crammed crosswise between others just like it, with a dead lawn the size of a postage stamp and cars parked bumper to bumper throughout the congested area. Bolan and Davis tried several times to elicit a response from within. Finally, the soldier had shrugged and kicked the door in. Davis had balked at that, for it was a bit too much like breaking and entering, but Bolan explained they could not be breaking into a home that was abandoned. He had taken note of the boarded windows, the litter coated with grime indicating time passed untouched and undisturbed. There was nobody home, all right, and there hadn't been for some time. The abandoned home smelled faintly of waste and mold, but there was no evidence of a crime.

Their third outing was more dangerous. The ramshackle home deep in some of the worst real estate in Detroit was essentially a safe house for some of the local gangs. They hadn't taken kindly to being disturbed. Bolan had been forced to draw both his weapons and make a show of his willingness to take down as many of the enemy as possible before he was gunned down. Only that show of strength had allowed Davis and Bolan to withdraw without incident. The soldier had even managed to question some of the gang members present as the two men were leaving, but they showed little interest in talk of knife attacks or the victims thereof. The Executioner would remember this address. When the current mission was over, he would be back with a plan—and the firepower needed to carry out that plan, whatever might be required. He had a long memory and no fondness for violent gangs.

Bolan was formulating a theory regarding the results of their scouting mission so far. That was why he had insisted he and Davis resume following the detective's annotated list of names. In doing so the soldier was gauging his liaison's reactions to what they encountered as much as he was testing his theory. There were many variables in play. What Davis said and did as they pursued the only strategy available to them would dictate what Bolan did in response. He wanted to avoid a full-scale onslaught among so many civilians, if he could help it. He would do whatever was necessary to prevent putting innocent lives at risk.

He had said as much to Davis as they drove the scarred but functional Crown Victoria into the heart of another neighborhood Davis described as "sketchy." When Bolan had cautioned the need for restraint, Davis had eyed him as if he could not believe what he had heard.

"You're packing a .44 Magnum gun and a machine pistol," he had said. "I'd hate to see what you consider a lack of restraint."

Bolan had let that go. It was a fair call, all things considered.

The apartment before which they presently stood was supposed to be occupied by the family of Henry Lipcomb. There was, they had been informed, no such person at that address. A great deal of profanity had accompanied that statement, followed by the slamming of the door. There was no reason necessarily to believe such a forceful denial. There was no reason to disbelieve it, either. That was, however, irrelevant. What occupied Bolan's attention most keenly were the sounds he was hearing inside the apartment.

The sound of the pump-action shotgun being racked was unmistakable.

The 12-gauge blew first one hole, then another through the door, but neither Davis nor Bolan was stupid enough to stand directly in front of it. The next blasts punched through peeling wallpaper and crumbling plaster on either side of the door frame. Davis backed off another half step, and Bolan could see it in his eyes: the detective was thinking about where he'd been standing before Bolan had urged him to move away.

The shotgunner inside fired and pumped his weapon in furious succession. Bolan counted off seven total rounds. There was a lull, which he gambled was the gunman reloading. Then he hit the door with all his weight.

The wreckage of the door gave way under him and he hit the floor beyond, crashing into and through a cheap pressboard coffee table. He landed beneath the gunman, who was struggling with a pistol-grip shotgun tricked out with a heat shield and a sidesaddle for ammunition. Bolan pushed off with one hand, continuing his sideways roll, and scissored his legs, toppling the man.

Bolan ripped the shotgun out of the man's grasp. The weapon's owner was a middle-aged Caucasian wearing a tracksuit. Gold rings flashed on his fingers; he held them up before his face, squalling, as Bolan reversed the shotgun and pointed it at him.

"Don't kill me! Don't kill me!"

The shot that rang out came from Davis's gun. Bolan had a moment's concern as he processed the sound and realized that Davis, behind him, just might have lined him up for the shot in an effort to remove Bolan from the equation. The shot was followed by another, and a third, as Davis tracked a figure moving quickly from the bathroom hallway to the kitchen.

"Behind you!" Davis shouted.

The shots that answered were from a larger weapon, probably a heavy revolver. Bolan jacked the pump on the shotgun, not knowing how many rounds the man on the floor had managed to load, and took aim. The shooter took cover behind the column supporting the kitchen doorway. Bolan blasted this with first one shot, then another, digging deep furrows in the wood and plaster with double-00 Buck.

The shotgun owner tried to make a break for it in the chaos. Davis caught him and hit him hard across the collarbone with the butt of the Glock. The two went down in a rolling, yelling pile of punches and knee strikes. Another salvo echoed from the kitchen.

Bolan emptied the shotgun into the plaster on his side of the dividing wall. He doubted he would be able to tag the enemy gunner, but that was not his purpose. He drove the shooter from cover instead, walking his 12-gauge rounds from left to right, chasing the figure into the open doorway.

The man was gaunt, wearing a T-shirt and a pair of shorts. Wild, stringy hair flew in all directions. The long barrel of his revolver, possibly a .44 Magnum, began to swing in Bolan's direction.

The Executioner released his grip on the recovered shotgun. He drew the Desert Eagle in a single, fluid motion. The barrel of the weapon came up before the shotgun hit the filthy living room carpet. Bolan pulled the trigger.

The shot punched a hole in the wild-haired man's sternum, cracking him open and dropping him to the floor. Bolan turned to assist Davis, but the detective already had the situation under control. He was kneeling on the back of the man wearing the tracksuit, reading him his rights.

Bolan, Desert Eagle in hand, checked the man he'd shot to make certain of him. There would be no miraculous healings there. He checked the kitchen, then the hallway and its closets. He checked the master bedroom and made sure to sweep the closet and shine his combat flashlight under the bed. There was nothing. When he got to the second bedroom, his eyes widened. He whistled.

The soldier went back into the living room and found Davis preparing to cuff his prisoner. He handed the detective one of the plastic zip-tie cuffs from his war bag. "Use that," he said.

"Thanks," Davis said. "It's impossible to get your cuffs back sometimes. I'd hate to lose another pair." He looked down at the zip-tie cuff and then back to Bolan. "I bet you go through a lot of these."

"Not as many as you might think," Bolan said.

"Touché," Davis said.

The detective, with Bolan's help, hauled the prisoner up onto the couch amid the garbage, old pizza boxes and other junk strewn about the room. Bolan stood over the seated man and pointed the Desert Eagle at the fellow's face.

"Name," Bolan said.

"Cole," the man said, turning pale. "Russ Cole. I live here, man."

"Identification," Bolan ordered.

"In my wallet, in my pocket," Cole said. "Jesus, man, don't kill me. I thought you were the competition, man! I didn't think there was any way you were really cops. I never would have pulled a trigger on a cop."

"Just a solid citizen, eh?" Davis said.

"Check the smaller bedroom," Bolan stated. Davis did as the soldier suggested and soon returned, hanging his head.

"Wow," he said. "I've never seen a setup quite that elaborate."

"It's actually a fairly elementary hydroponic float system," Bolan told him. "Three kiddie pools full of water. They'd add nutrients to it as needed. If we check the closet in there, we'll probably find whatever they've been using. From the looks of it, they've got an inverter set up to handle the juice from the bank of car batteries stacked by the wall. The lights over the plants are LEDs. They don't generate much waste heat."

"Smart," Davis said. "The department checks regularly for reports of irregularly high electrical usage. Occasionally we sweep suspect neighborhoods with infrared equipment for heat signatures. This wouldn't trip either of those. At least, I don't think it would."

"Which means it was just the bad luck of these two," Bolan said, jerking his chin at first the dead man and then the prisoner, "that they thought we were rival pot dealers come to claim their grow house."

Cole looked confused. "You guys are cops, ain't you?"

Bolan looked at him. "Shut up." He holstered the Desert Eagle.

"You don't have a brother who was killed in an unsolved stabbing, do you?" Davis said, sounding resigned.

"Huh?" Cole said. "No, man. I had a cousin who was shanked in County. He got out last year, though. This about that? He do something?"

"No," Bolan said. "And it wasn't about your marijuana science project in there, either."

"Shit," Cole said.

"Yeah," Bolan told him. In his pocket, he felt his phone vibrate. He moved beyond Cole's field of vision, into the grimy kitchen, and checked the device. Stony Man Farm had uploaded several files to the secure smartphone, indicated by a blinking icon on its screen.

He checked through them. Most were supporting data on the men whose photos he had sent for identification. Each file was tagged with a green halo, which meant the initial suspicions Aaron "the Bear" Kurtzman's cyberteam had were borne out in more thorough analysis. It was, of course, Kurtzman and his people who executed Price's mission directives.

There was another set of files, these messages from Brognola. They were notes, really, and they indicated just which local power brokers and law-enforcement officials Brognola or his office had bullied, begged, bargained with, or otherwise influenced. It would be useful information if things got worse, which they most certainly would. The inclusion of this information was Brognola's hint that Bolan should remind those locally of conversations that had already taken place and sabers that had already been rattled in the bureaucratic halls of power. It would help keep Brognola off the phone any more than absolutely necessary in the hours to come.

Bolan hoped that wasn't wishful thinking on Brognola's part. One never knew. He stowed the phone.

Davis called for backup. The shots fired so far were considerable, but Bolan was not surprised when Davis reported there had been no calls to emergency services from the building. They would wait long enough for Davis's fellow officers to collect their prisoner and begin going through the apartment for evidence. Representatives from the DEA would be called, as well. That was all standard procedure.

When the situation was under control, they returned to the unmarked cruiser. Davis fired up the engine and pulled out into traffic without saying anything. When he finally spoke, he sounded dispirited.

"What's our next move?"

"Do you think we're getting anywhere like this?" Bolan asked.

The detective looked crestfallen. "Cooper, I don't understand. I checked the files in our database when I did my research. These are the names and the addresses that we have in the system. These are the department's own files."

"The department's files are obviously wrong," Bolan said.

"But that's impossible."

"Is it? Are you that sure?"

Davis took a moment to consider that. "Well, of course they're not…infallible. But these aren't minor errors. They're complete non sequiturs. It's as if the list is linking us to completely unrelated cases, to random people."

"Or to addresses selected to throw us off the track," Bolan said.

"Us?"

"Anyone," Bolan said. "Anyone who might be tempted to go back and look through the files. Anyone trying to identify a pattern in the knifings."

"You're back to a menace within the department again," Davis said. "I really don't like to think of that as a serious possibility."

"But you'll have to."

"Yeah," Davis said. "The only thing we can do is go back to the department and check the computer. I'm not exactly an amateur when it comes to that. I worked in Records for a year when I was coming up. Now that I know what to look for, I'll bet I can find it. If there's anything to find."

"There will be," Bolan told him.

Davis had his own office in the Detroit police building where he was stationed. This was not the mark of distinction that one might think it to be, Davis had explained on the way over. He had driven the battered cruiser capably and with a heavy foot, perhaps energized by the idea of getting to the bottom of a mess he thought was making him look bad. He was young enough still, Bolan thought, that he took it personally. Maybe he thought that Agent Cooper was looking down on him for his failure. That was if the failure was unintentional, not something planned to screen the fact that Davis was working with the opposition. The soldier did not believe that to be the case. He did not accept that someone who had shown the mettle Davis had thus far demonstrated could be a traitor, a dirty cop. But Mack Bolan had not lived as long as he had, while fighting his endless war, by giving his trust fully or easily.

Davis's place of employment, for most of cops at his rank, was a bull pen of desks in a large, open area on the second floor of a badly aging, seventies-era multistory building downtown. The decor of the office had not been updated since the seventies, and the space—intended to look "mod" and sleek decades earlier—just looked tired and threadbare.

This was fairly typical of working station houses in Bolan's experience, and he did not hold it against the building's occupants. Men and women of law enforcement, especially in high-crime areas, did toiled at difficult, risky and mostly thankless jobs.

Davis explained that there simply was not enough room to wedge yet another desk into the bull pen. As the junior-most detective assigned here, then, he was given his own private so-called office shoehorned into what had been a storage closet adjacent to the open floor space. More than one officer, including the lower-ranking uniformed ones, commented on this as Davis made his way through the building with Bolan in tow. "Hey, party at Davis's place" was the most frequent taunt.

Davis took all this in stride, and the ribbing seemed good-natured as far as Bolan could tell. He led the soldier to his office, moved a stack of books on the second chair wedged into the space and invited him to sit down. Bolan left the door open and watched the hallway as Davis booted his computer.

The detective bumped the bookcase against the wall as he worked. He did not seem to notice each time his elbow came in contact with the textbooks there. Bolan scanned the titles; they were obviously from a college career spent pursuing criminal science. Had there been any free wall space not covered by the door when it was open, Bolan imagined that Davis might have hung his diploma there.

Davis muttered to himself as he worked. He was searching through the list, Bolan gathered. He also seemed to be checking that list against the source files from which the names were drawn. He did not seem satisfied in what he was finding. As the younger man worked, the soldier kept his attention fixed on the hallway outside. Something was nagging at him, some feeling of anticipation. He realized, then, what it was. The officers passing by Davis's closet were looking in with something strange in their expressions. On most of the men, it was a morbid sort of curiosity, as if they expected something bad to have befallen Detective Davis. On a few, it was almost disappointment, as if the expected bad news was not forthcoming and it was something they considered a loss.

If they think something bad is going down, Bolan thought, then it's only a matter of time before—

There was a knocking on the door frame.

There were three men standing in the doorway. Two of them were detectives, their shirts rumpled, ties at half-mast. The tall one, his features creased with a lived-in scowl, wore an equally rumpled gray trench coat as if he thought he was the star of a detective noir movie. The short, fatter one, who was balding and trying to cover it up with a comb-over, had a jowly face dominated by deeply set, hostile eyes. The third man was a young uniformed officer with a flattop buzz cut.

"Hey," the fat one said. "Looks like little Adam's got a buddy. Hello, buddy." There was no mirth in the man's tone. He leaned on the door frame with what he probably thought was calculated menace. Bolan eyed him curiously.

"Slate," Davis said. He sounded tired, as if Slate were someone whose presence he were tolerating under protest. "Agent Cooper of the Justice Department, meet Detective Brian Slate. His tall friend is Detective Bill Griffith. I'm afraid I don't know the name of the officer with them."

"Glase," the uniformed officer said. "Tim Glase."

"Nice to meet you," Davis said. He did not sound very sincere.

"Yeah, yeah," Slate said, brushing Glase's hand out of the way. He pointed a thick index finger at Bolan. "You, pretty boy," he said, dropping any pretense of civility. "You've been pokin' your nose in where it don't belong. You may think you're pretty hot shit back in Washington or wherever. But we're real cops here. We don't need your kind muckin' about."

Bolan said nothing. He remained in his seat, surveying

both Griffith and Slate, wondering if Glase was hanging back out of some kind of strategy or simply because he deferred to the other two. Bolan was an apt and experienced student of human nature. Their words, their body language, and their choices of conversational tacks were all pieces of data to Bolan, who was studying them as a lion might study its next meal.

"He thinks he's some kind of computer expert," Griffith said. His hands were in his pockets. Bolan watched him closely. "He thinks he can out-detective senior detectives."

"Look, you two," Davis said, apparently judging Glase beneath notice, "I'm a little tired of this game. You've done your hazing. You've had your fun. We're all cops here. I have work to do, and you're interrupting an agent of the Justice Department while on official duty. Please go."

Griffith and Slate traded expressions of mock awe. "Well, well," Slate said. "That sounds damned official. Maybe I should put it another way, little boy," he said. His voice grew harsher, and there was no joking in it, even by the lame standards of humor that amused someone like him. "I'm not asking you, kid. I'm telling you. You're going to conclude that your investigation is going nowhere. So a few losers got stabbed. Detroit is full of crime. You need to focus on something a little more productive. Like right now."

"And you," Griffith said, poking Bolan in the chest, "are out of your league, pal. Go back to your boyfriend in the big city, if you have one, or whatever bathhouse you hang out in, and find somebody else to do. Davis here already has a top bunk. He's spoken for by us."

Davis looked irritated. Bolan looked down at the finger poking him in the chest.

He looked up, slowly, at Griffith, his eyes full of cold, blue lethality.

"So, uh," Griffith said, "you're, uh, gonna leave town. Like, soonest."

Bolan looked down at the finger again, then back up at Griffith. "Take your hand off me."

Something about that made Slate angry. His face turned red. "You listen good, you asshole," he began. "If my partner says jump, you say—"

Bolan struck, as quick as a rattlesnake. He grabbed Griffith's index finger and squeezed his hand into a fist. Griffith's finger snapped with an audible crack.

"Oh my God!" Slate blurted. His hand disappeared into his jacket, going for his gun.

Bolan wasn't finished. He opened his hand, positioned his fingers on the stricken Griffith's wrist and twisted in and down. The detective went to his knees in front of Bolan's chair. Simultaneously, the soldier snapped a kick, still seated, from the knee, catching Slate just behind his own knee joint. The leg buckled and Slate lost his balance, toppling forward. The Executioner shifted slightly in his chair, grabbed the back of Slate's head as the man pitched over, and slammed the fat detective's nose against the wooden lip of the chair.

Blood spurted from Slate's nose. Bolan gave him a shove, planting him in the corridor beyond on his ample posterior. He sat there in a sitting position, his gun forgotten, grabbing at his nose and bleating like a sheep.

"By...by noge!" he said through the blood and his broken beak. *"You broge my noge!"*

Bolan twirled Griffith's captured wrist, torquing the man over so that he faced the corridor. He kicked Griffith in the butt, sending him sprawling. He landed amid the drops of blood still leaking from Slate's face.

Glase had his hand on his holstered sidearm. "You, sir, just assaulted a pair of Detroit's finest," he announced. "I'm going to have to put you under arrest."

Bolan shrugged aside his leather jacket so the butt of his Beretta was visible. He very slowly, deliberately put his hand on the weapon. "You want to take me in, kid," he said, "you're going to need more than a trumped up charge backed by a pair of dirty cops."

"Hey!" Griffith protested. "You can't say that!"

"He just did," Davis said. Bolan looked over. The detective had his Glock out and was covering the three men. "Now get the hell out of here, all three of you. If anybody goes filing any reports, I just might have to remember a few irregularities in some of the fine casework I know you two sad sacks have worked. Nobody sees anything around here," he reminded them. "Unless they do."

Slate managed to stumble to his feet, his nose still streaming blood. He pulled a handkerchief from his pocket and pushed it at his bent nose, trying to mop up the mess. Griffith cradled his hand and shot Davis and Bolan a hateful look.

"You're dead," he said. "Both of you. You're fucking *dead men*."

Bolan stared him down. He said nothing in response. He snapped open the retaining strap on his shoulder holster.

"Go, go," Slate said through his bubbling, bloody nose. The three men retreated.

Bolan reached up calmly and snapped his holster shut. "You find anything?" he asked Davis.

Davis looked at him. "You just…you just beat up two men while sitting in a chair. With one hand."

Bolan waved that away. "I said, did you find anything?"

Davis blinked. "Cooper," he said, "I don't know what kind of pull you think you have in Washington, but it may not be enough for two like that."

"You keep forgetting the third guy," Bolan said.

"I'm serious, Cooper," Davis said. "You know as well as I do that rumors float around the force. There are some who say those two have murdered suspects in the past and covered it up. That they're on the take from the Mafia."

"I'd say that's pretty much a given, wouldn't you?" Bolan said. "Why else would they be leaning on us? The Mafia just fielded a football team or two trying to put bullets in our heads. The attempt has failed. Now these two just coincidentally show up to tell me to get out of Dodge and throw a scare into you. You don't have to be good at math to put these numbers together and come up with dirty cop."

"Can you call in some backup, Cooper?" Davis said. "I've done what I can, and I'll keep doing that. But with Slate and Griffith breathing down our necks we may be facing a new level of difficulty here."

"And you were offended that I thought you might be dirty," Bolan said.

"Low blow, Cooper," Davis said. "Low blow."

"It gets better," Bolan said. "I was bluffing."

"What?"

"You need to know something," Bolan said. "I won't kill a cop, if it comes to that."

"You…you broke a cop's nose and a cop's finger!"

"They'll heal."

"Cooper, you mean to tell me that if Slate or Griffith meant to shoot you—or *me*—you would let them do it?"

"I won't kill a cop," Bolan said. "Not even a dirty one, if I can help it."

"That's very comforting, Cooper." Davis sighed.

"Now that we've gotten the bad news out of the way," Bolan said, "did you find anything?"

"Well, that's where things get interesting," Davis said. "All of our files are indexed with a file number. The file numbers and the information, things like addresses, relevant information, and the like, are kept in separate fields in the database. It's why we have to abbreviate so much that it's almost shorthand, because the fields are only so big."

Bolan nodded. "And?"

"Somebody did a relatively crude job of swapping out the file numbers and the case data," Davis said. "They didn't hide it very well. I checked the master database that tracks file

numbers by date entered. Using that I was able to find the
files that those numbers were supposed to go with, instead
of the ones they are paired with now. It was a one-to-one
replacement, not something that sent me hunting among multiple files."

"Meaning…" Bolan prompted.

"Meaning that whoever wanted to throw off an investigation into the knife killings didn't try very hard to do it. They
just made sure the case numbers each led to a single dead
end. Basically they assigned the wrong names, the wrong addresses, or both, to the file backup data I researched. Once
I knew which file numbers to look for, I was able to find the
one that was supposed to be matched to it. It was a simple set
of crossed wires."

"So whoever did this didn't think anyone was going to
look too hard."

"Cooper?"

"Think about it," Bolan said. "If they thought a deep look
was likely, they would have taken more time. Careers are on
the line here. Prison time, possibly. Life and death. Yet they
did a simple file switch that you found in minutes."

"Well," Davis said. "I'm not an amateur."

"Trust me," Bolan said, thinking of Kurtzman and his
team of computer specialists at the Farm, "you may not be
a rank amateur, but I know people worlds better at this than
you. A real investigation would involve personnel like that.
So the way these files were hidden tells us something."

"What?" Davis asked.

"Power," Bolan said. "The arrogance of power. The person
or persons behind this think they'll be able to deal with
anyone who does stumble across this information."

"By hiring Mafia hit men to ice them?"

"Yeah," Bolan nodded. "Just like that."

Davis tapped a few more keys. "You'd better escort me to
the shared printer," he told Bolan. "Although I hate to make

you get up out of your chair to do it. There might be some angry, wounded detectives waiting out there."

"There might, at that."

Davis paused to close the door and lock his little closet. "I'm in deep shit on this, Cooper," he said quietly. "Slate and Griffith have a lot of friends in this place."

The two men walked to the printer. Davis retrieved the list data, finally corrected. They were, unfortunately, starting from scratch, at least insofar as finding the source of the knife killings was concerned. Bolan, however, was impressed with what they had managed to shake loose so far. Even the misdirection that had begun this little escapade was itself a hint at the source of the corruption and crime here in Detroit.

Davis made a detour once they were near the printer. He stopped to talk to an attractive young woman at one of the computer stations in the adjacent records processing area. Bolan wasn't sure what that was about, but the exchange was brief. Davis might simply have been flirting for all he knew. The detective returned quickly enough and grabbed his printout.

"Come with me," Bolan said when Davis had folded and pocketed his sheaf of papers.

"Where are we going?" Davis asked.

"To see your lieutenant."

"Oh, boy. Try not to gouge out his eye or something."

They paused at Sumner's office just long enough for Bolan to walk up to the man's desk. "Lieutenant Sumner," Bolan said. "I'm lodging a formal complaint."

"Oh?" Sumner said. "About what?" He was a tall man, in good shape. He stood toe-to-toe with Bolan, separated from the soldier by only his desk. He did not look cowed in any way. Bolan admired that. He hoped the man wasn't dirty.

"Griffith and Slate," Bolan said.

A shadow crossed Sumner's features. Those names, Bolan concluded, didn't bring Sumner a great deal of pleasure. That meant the lieutenant wasn't stupid. He knew, or suspected, what was going on in his domain.

"They're clumsy," Bolan said. "Had a little accident outside Davis's office. Whoever waxes that floor should put out a sign."

"Waxes that floor…" Sumner said. "You've got to be kidding me."

"It's a hazard," Bolan said. "Those two are lucky to have gotten out of it with only some minor damage. A broken finger and nose. Next time, it might be much more serious." He paused and gave Sumner a hard stare. "I wouldn't want to have to call Washington about this. My boss can be very unpleasant when he's interrupted."

"Yeah," Sumner said. He was quiet, surrendering without saying the words. "Yeah, I bet. I'll keep it in mind."

"Good," Bolan said. He turned and left. Davis followed.

"You're making friends fast around here," he said.

"I believe in burning my bridges as I get to them," Bolan said.

"Explains a lot," Davis said.

Those who lived in affluent neighborhoods, in gated communities, in big houses hidden by landscaping and distance from the seedier elements around them, never really understood something that was essential to Bolan's knowledge of human predation. There was no rich suburb in the world, no wealthy district, no beautiful area that was not within walking or driving distance of a festering pesthole that bred crime. There were those, Bolan knew, who said the key to avoiding danger was to be passive, to avoid everywhere that bad things were presumed to happen. If you did not live in a "bad neighborhood," if you did not go to or through one, why, you could avoid most if not all of the random violence that might otherwise affect you in modern society.

This was dangerously foolish.

Bolan understood violence intimately. He had made combating violence with greater, more focused, more righteous violence his life's work. He knew that violence, that predators, could find anyone, anywhere. Shirley Kingsley was proof of that. As Bolan and Davis sat on the floral couch in her living room, drinking coffee she had made for them, tears ran down Mrs. Kingsley's face.

Shirley Kingsley was a widow.

Her home was in a gated community only a few minutes' drive from the abandoned slums where Bolan and Davis had only so recently been fighting for their lives. Mrs. Kingsley had no idea that scores of Mafia gunners had died in Detroit within the past few hours. She would be aghast if anyone told her. As it was, Bolan was curious to know why news of the shootings had not made the local media. He wondered if Brognola, the Farm, or both were behind that. It was also possible that the shootings of what could only be known criminals weren't lead story material, given that serial knifings promised to be much juicier. And the first news reports could not be far away, given what Brognola and the Farm had told him in his mission briefing.

"What bothers me most," Mrs. Kingsley was saying, "is the senselessness of it. Norman was a good man. I don't believe the poor dear had ever had an exciting thought in his whole life. He inherited money. We lived well, and peacefully. Even in death he provided for me. I've never wanted for anything. He was such a sweet, kind, generous man. I think about how awfully, how violently he died, and it hurts me so badly."

Bolan's heart went out to the woman. He, too, carried his battle losses with him. Those losses were seldom just.

"Did your husband have any reason to believe he might be targeted, Mrs. Kingsley?" Davis asked. He placed his coffee cup gently on the saucer provided for him.

"Targeted?" Kingsley asked.

"As for...forgive me, ma'am, assassination," Davis explained. "Any reason someone would want to kill him. Him, specifically."

"Oh, heavens, no," Kingsley said.

"No threats were made that you can recall?" Bolan asked. "Any odd encounters he might have experienced?"

"I'm not sure I understand." Mrs. Kingsley shook her head.

"If he were chosen specifically," Bolan said, "rather than randomly, he might have encountered his murderer beforehand. He may have been marked, so to speak, by the killer."

Mrs. Kingsley put her own cup down and folded her hands in her lap. "No," she said. "Nothing like that happened, or if it did, Norman didn't tell me. I suppose he might have kept something like that from me for fear of worrying me, but he was generally quite honest. I'm afraid I don't know of anything like that."

"Thank you for your time, Mrs. Kingsley," Bolan said. "I apologize for putting you through this. I know this is not easy."

"Thank you, young man," she said. "Good luck to you both. I hope you find whoever did it. I truly do."

"We will," Davis promised.

They left, shown out by a housekeeper who regarded them suspiciously. Bolan nodded to her as they made for the carefully landscaped street.

"Random," Davis said. "She thinks it was completely random."

"And it may have been," Bolan said. "We don't have enough data to make that decision, not yet. But we're at least finally talking to the right people."

"You don't strike me as the talking type, overall," Davis said.

"I'm not," Bolan said. "I'm the make-things-happen type, which is why I'm not surprised to see *him* there." Bolan pointed.

The marked police cruiser passing slowly by began to accelerate. The driver had a flattop crew cut.

"Come on," Bolan said. "Keys."

Davis tossed him the car keys without argument and Bolan took the wheel. The engine roared in response to his turn of the key. He pressed the pedal full to the floor.

"What is it?" Davis asked.

"The driver," Bolan said, as they cleared the development's open gate at full speed, drawing shouts from the gate guard. Ahead of them, the police cruiser switched on its lights and sirens, heading toward the city and thicker traffic. "He was that uniform backing up your buddies Slate and Griffith."

"He followed us?" Davis asked.

"Unless coincidence extends to the department dispatching a vehicle to the same affluent neighborhood to do nothing but drive by and then speed away when noticed," Bolan said.

"I had you pegged as someone with no sense of humor, Cooper," Davis said, deadpan.

"Comes with the job," Bolan said. The cruiser's engine growled and the Crown Victoria shot forward between two slower-moving vehicles.

The marked car led them on quite a chase. Bolan, an experienced wheelman himself, was forced to employ many tricks to keep up. The cop car had the advantage of an official presence in its lights and sirens.

Bolan reached out and switched on the cruiser's own lights and sirens. There was no dash-mounted unit; the lights were concealed in the grille. The unmarked Crown Victoria chased its white-and-blue-striped counterpart through red lights and across tight intersections.

"He might start shooting," Davis said. His hand drifted toward his holstered gun.

"I don't think so," Bolan said. "If he had intended to take a shot at us he would have done so already. Slate and Griffith wouldn't have braced us and made threats if something more severe were planned. No, he was sent to keep an eye on us when we made it clear we were looking for a fight."

Davis was silent for a long moment. He grimaced occasionally as the car came dangerously close to another vehicle. Bolan was very careful to avoid pedestrians, but there were times when he was surprised himself that he did not clip the car's mirrors off as he shot between other moving vehicles.

"Cooper," Davis said, "it's as if you calculated the benefit of injuring those two specifically to elicit a response."

Bolan said nothing. The kid was smart. He allowed himself the ghost of a grin.

"There." The soldier pointed. "He's taking that side street. Hold on."

Bolan punched the accelerator and ripped the wheel to the side, forcing the car through a powered slide as its rear-wheel drive pushed it through a rubber-burning, skidding, squealing arc. The rear of the car clipped a light pole, but not badly. Davis looked back, then forward, and saw the trash bins.

"Uh-oh," he said.

The bins were heavy-gauge steel and huge, designed to be moved by sanitation trucks or not at all. There was very little room to maneuver. Bolan whipped the wheel left, then right, the nose and the tail of the car clipping brick facade with each adjustment. Sparks flew. He clipped first one trash bin, then another, always just on the edge of losing control.

The marked police car stayed ahead of them, but Bolan's expert handling of the powerful cruiser was closing the gap. Officer Glase would be getting desperate by this point, using all his best moves and seeing Bolan's lights flashing in his rearview mirror no matter what he tried. The trick was to pressure him in a way that didn't send him dangerously close to pedestrians. Bolan used the nose of the car to urge Glase this way and that, nudging him with his presence alone, using the specter of the pursuit car to prod Glase in a direction leading him toward less population density.

"It gets pretty industrial up here," Davis said, nodding in the direction Bolan was herding Glase.

"I know." Bolan said. "I remember. It's not my first trip to Detroit."

"No?" Davis said. "How long?"

"Been a while," Bolan said vaguely.

They shifted left, then right. Cars surrounded them. One

of them, ahead, spun out as Glase sideswiped it. Bolan veered around the car. He nodded to the radio, but Davis was already reaching for it. The detective called in the accident.

"You want me to call in backup?" he asked.

"We're already chasing a Detroit police car," Bolan said. "We don't know who we can trust and who we can't." He couldn't spare Davis a meaningful glance, but the detective could probably hear the gravity in his voice.

As they drove they monitored the police band; if Glase was calling in help, he wasn't doing it over the marked car's radio. Bolan kept tight to the other man's tail until the two cars' bumpers were practically touching. That's when Glase tried to get tricky.

Glase hit the brakes. It was the obvious move and Bolan was waiting for it. He accelerated to meet the bright red lights. The push bars mounted to the front of the unmarked vehicle rammed the bumper, doing little more than trading paint. The momentum shoved Glase's vehicle forward.

"Pursuit Intervention Technique," Davis said.

"I don't often hear the PIT maneuver referred to that way," Bolan said. "But no, I don't want to force him off the road. I want him scared."

"More deliberate manipulation?"

Bolan said nothing. He was too focused on his driving.

Glase turned hard right and rammed through the chain-link fence outside a freight yard. Beyond the fence, rows of trailers waited. Huge metal containers, of the type carried by flatbeds and transferred to cargo ships, were also arrayed and stacked here. Glase had to be nearly standing on his cruiser's accelerator as he tried to lose himself among the trailers.

"Do you know this area?" Bolan asked.

"No," Davis said. "Not specifically. I couldn't say if there's another way out or not."

"We'll just have to wing it," Bolan said. He slowed the car. They made a cautious circuit of the freight yard. Bolan kept one eye on the mirror at all times. He warned Davis to keep watch over the entrance, while trying to angle their own vehicle to block any straight path back the way they had come.

"There!" Davis shouted, pointing.

The police cruiser was gunning past them. Bolan jammed on the brakes, threw Davis's unmarked vehicle in Reverse and burned rubber in the opposite direction. The maneuver he was contemplating would be tricky to time.

As Glase neared the bottleneck that was the opening in the fence, Bolan turned the wheel. The rear of the Crown Victoria circled and bashed the flank of the police cruiser, driving it just far enough to the right to cause Glase to slam into a concrete-anchored support pole. A section of fence crashed down on the spiderwebbed windshield. The engine raced, critically damaged.

Bolan was out of the car before it had stopped moving fully, throwing the gearshift into Park almost as an afterthought. He drew his Desert Eagle; the firepower it offered would easily punch through most of the police cruiser. Davis followed as backup, deferring to Bolan's play.

"Don't move!" the Executioner shouted. "Step out of the car!"

Glase didn't move. Bolan stepped closer. The officer could be shamming, waiting to pull a weapon at the last minute. Bolan did not intend to give the crooked cop a chance to put a bullet in him.

"I think he's unconscious," Davis said.

"Cover me," Bolan said. "It could be a trick." He reached in through the open driver's window and gave Glase a shove. The man moaned. He had hit the steering wheel, and there was a light gash on his forehead.

Bolan opened the car door and grabbed Glase by the shoulders, aware that at any moment a knife or a gun could appear. Glase made no hostile moves. It was clear, after a few moments, that he was out of it. Bolan arranged him in a sitting position on the pavement, using the crumpled fender of the police cruiser as a backrest.

"I'll get the first-aid kit," Davis said. Bolan nodded.

The soldier crouched near the officer, his Desert Eagle held firmly in his right hand. "Glase," he said. "Wake up."

Glase muttered something. Davis came back with the kit and applied a bandage to the man's forehead, while Bolan kept the officer under his gun. He snapped his fingers in front of Glase's face a few times. The officer's eyes finally focused and he shook himself like wet dog.

"Try not to move too much," Bolan said. "I just might put a bullet in you to settle you down."

Glase's expression hardened when he realized he was staring down the barrel of a pistol. He moved, suddenly, as if jerking for the door of the car behind him. Bolan could see the barrel of a shotgun mounted between the front seats. He grabbed Glase by the shoulder and shoved him back down.

"Get off me!" Glase spit. "I'll kill you, I'll kill your family—"

Bolan balled his left fist and punched Glase in the cheekbone, hard. Glase's head snapped back. Normally, the Executioner would not risk a closed-fist punch to an opponent's mouth; getting someone else's teeth caught in your knuckles could lead to infection and diminished combat readiness. With Glase more or less frozen in position, he calculated his shot for maximum effect and minimum risk.

Glase sputtered and opened his mouth to speak again. Bolan grabbed him by the hair with his free hand and bounced the officer's head off the side of the police car.

"Cooper," Davis began.

Bolan was not out of control; he simply needed to establish, with Glase, who was in control, and establish it firmly. Interrogations, or, in this case, messages were about power relationships. One had to seize the initiative immediately and then keep it if one's goals were to be achieved.

"You listen to me," Bolan said. He shoved the barrel of the Desert Eagle into the spot where he'd punched Glase, pressing just hard enough to make the weapon's presence known. "The only reason I'm not boring a .44-sized hole through your brain right now, punk, is that I want you to carry a message. I want you to go back to whoever sent you. I want you to tell them we spotted you and we owned you from the moment we put eyes on you. I want you to tell them that justice is coming. You got that? Say it."

Glase looked at him blankly. "Say it!"

"Justice," Glase repeated. "Justice is coming."

"Good," Bolan said. He stood, hauling Glase to his feet, and gave the officer a hard shove. The crooked cop staggered but stayed upright. "Start running!" Bolan ordered.

Glase looked back at him, and something in Bolan's face was sufficiently convincing. He ran, his gait unsteady, his pace hastened by what had to be true fear.

"You've done that before," Davis said. "I thought you didn't kill cops?"

"I have, and I don't. Usually," Bolan said. "But he doesn't know that."

A crackle of static from the radio in Glase's cruiser contained the words "knife" and "assault." Bolan looked at it. Davis hurried over and stuck his head in the open doorway.

"Cooper!" he shouted. "We've got a report of a possible attack. Right now!"

"In progress?" Bolan asked.

"In progress!" Davis said.

They ran for the Ford.

9

Patrick Farnham threw the knife, a cheap Chinese "combat" model, onto the ground. Buying a box of the knives had been his innovation, something none of the others had thought of before. They were inexpensive enough to buy in bulk, and they were sharp enough to be deadly.

It was a question of honor. A brother of the blade was defined by his weapon as much as the technique he used to wield it, for without the knife, what was he? A common brawler and little else. Patrick Farnham was no common brawler. He sought the enlightenment that only lethal combat with a knife could teach him, an enlightenment that was everything. It was his obsession. It was his passion. It was his reason. No one could understand, and no one would understand. But that was not their fault. At least, that was not the fault of most people. It was just that Farnham knew something these *mundanes*, these vanilla people, these sheep, did not.

Farnham had never been closer to death. And thus it was that Farnham truly appreciated life…and wanted to understand it while he could.

His had been a relatively ordinary life, once. He looked back on himself of years gone by and was appalled by the sleeping fool he had once been. He had been so complacent, so unaware of the rapidity with which everything could change, the way everything could be lost in a few heartbeats.

He had gone to high school in Detroit and managed to graduate. He had tried college, briefly, but it was not for him. He found classes boring, though he was intelligent enough to do well if he wished. And he was aware of that. He just could not waste his time sitting in any more classrooms.

He had sought work in the factories of Detroit, but jobs were harder and harder to come by as more and more manufacturing went overseas. He had struggled for some time, working through temporary staffing companies, picking up seasonal work where he could, never really knowing from week to week if he was going to have enough money to pay the rent on his miserable apartment.

"Pick up the knife," he said. The middle-aged man he had cornered in the shadows of the parking garage looked at the blade in terror. He was dressed well. He might be a banker or something, the type of person once called a "yuppie." The car he'd been trying to get to, the car before which Farnham presently stood, was a BMW. Here in Detroit that was more of a statement than it might be elsewhere. But Farnham had not chosen this man for any reason of class or wealth-conscience. He did not intend to rob him. Farnham was no thief.

Farnham was a duelist.

He hated that he had not always known it. He hated that he owed others, others who had proved to be unworthy, for this discovery. It bothered him because he believed he should have been strong enough to come to it on his own. They would always be able to hold that over him. Even if he killed every last one of them, he would know. He would take that knowledge to his grave.

He had been working, really just existing, and occasionally taking classes at a karate dojo down the block. It was there that he met a man who stilled trained there, a high-ranking student who had been with the school for some time and made occasional trips back. That man was Reginald Chamblis, and Farnham had known the man for several weeks before he realized that this was the same Chamblis whose name appeared regularly in the business section of the newspapers.

Chamblis took little notice of Farnham, and Farnham took little notice of him.

Then, everything changed.

He had gone to the doctor for headaches. He had always had them, but they got so bad that finally, during one of those rare times when he had health insurance, he took advantage of it to see a specialist.

He was told he had a brain tumor and that it would kill him.

Farnham could not believe it. He was young, in the prime of his life. He was in great physical condition. He took good care of himself despite a somewhat irregular diet and schedule. He had done nothing wrong. Hell, he thought, he had done nothing at all. Nothing in life.

And then it hit him that the death sentence he had been given was not a death sentence at all, but a life sentence.

He began trying things he had always thought of doing, but never did. He went to wild nightclubs he had always thought of visiting. He tried drugs he had never had the courage to take. He asked beautiful women to go home with him, never dreaming they would accept, and they responded to him. He had a confidence born of having nothing to lose, and the urgency that came with knowing that one's time was finite.

In his martial-arts training he fought with more reckless abandon than ever before, challenging students of much higher rank and ability. He fought with such ferocity that he won, and when he lost, he reveled in the pain that told him he was still alive.

Chamblis noticed.

Chamblis saw the change in him. He invited Farnham to take special lessons at his private studio. From the moment he first picked up a knife, Farnham was hooked. He loved the discipline of the blade. He adored its power. He admired its lethality. He obsessed over its immediacy. For with a blade in hand, a man could live or die with a single thrust, cut, or block. The knife became Farnham's whole world.

The brain tumor, with treatment, eventually abated. The doctors had been wrong. Farnham was going to live. But in believing himself to be doomed, he had discovered the key to a life worth having. He took many lives as part of Chamblis's group, and thanks to the group's rules, he was never in any danger of being caught.

And then everything changed again.

His headaches came back. He ignored them for as long as he could, but they got so bad that he had no choice but to seek a doctor's help. He needed prescription painkillers at the very least. The doctor told him what he feared most.

His tumor was back.

Possibly it had never been gone. Possibly it had gone into remission, only to reassert itself at some future point. Farnham would never know. He knew only that, unlike the first time, the headaches never got better. The tumor was slowly destroying him from within his own mind. He had no idea how much time he had.

What might be a week or a month could also be fifty years; there was just no way to tell. Farnham's sense of urgency returned, only worse. Suddenly, Chamblis's rules about dueling only those members of society whom no one would miss seemed like a pointless waste of precious, precious time.

How else could someone truly know if his skill passed muster unless he fought more than street trash? Any human being one encountered could conceivably have the ability to understand the discipline of the blade. Those individuals, if they were to be found, would not be found among the dregs of humanity—drug addicts, prostitutes, the homeless.

Farnham wanted to challenge real people. People who hadn't given up. People who understood that their lives had value. People who would fight to keep those lives.

It made all the difference in the world. When he threw one of his disposable knives at a prospective mark, he knew that if that man or woman picked it up, he would be fighting a vibrant living human being who wanted, more than anything, to live. That made the duels that much sweeter. That made them so much more powerful. If Farnham was to understand life and its mysteries before the tumor killed him, he had to keep testing himself against *real* people.

He had never told Chamblis about the brain tumor. He could not risk that; Chamblis was just ruthless enough that he might see that tumor as the risk of discovery. He might wonder if a brain-addled Farnham, on his death bed, would suddenly begin telling fever dreams of dueling cults. Farnham had no intention of being taken out that way. He would go by his own hand or in an honorable duel. That was the life and the death that he sought.

He had so much work to do first.

It was crazy, of course. The old Farnham would have thought the idea of seeking self-knowledge, or cosmic knowledge, or any knowledge through mortal combat to be absurd. But the old Farnham had known nothing about mortality. Mortality, the new Farnham understood beyond all else.

Chamblis, of course, had not understood Farnham's urgency. Farnham had hoped to convince him that dueling the leftovers of society was passing up the best that the discipline of the blade had to offer. Chamblis would not hear of it. He had ordered Farnham to stop. He had threatened to excommunicate Farnham from the fellowship of the knife.

There had been a student in Chamblis's studio whom Farnham had always despised. The man's name was Byron. Byron thought he was much braver, much tougher, much better with a knife than he truly was. When no one else was around but Byron and another student, Byron enjoyed telling that student how inferior he was compared to himself. It was an annoying habit borne of arrogance. None of the others had seen fit to bring it up to Chamblis, probably because none of them wanted to duel Byron. Dueling the man would be the very solution Chamblis applied to a dispute among members of his group.

With nothing to lose and wonderful insight to gain, Farnham had waited until he was alone with Byron in the studio. Then he had drawn his blades and announced, simply, that he was going to gut Byron like a fish.

Poor Byron did not put up nearly the fight he had always promised to. Farnham's exhilaration at winning quickly gave way to the realization that Chamblis would not look fondly on this act. He would not want a dead man in the middle of his studio, most certainly. He might suggest a duel among his students, but in his own way he would control the outcome, would control the circumstances. That was Chamblis's way. He would be angry when he learned of this.

Farnham had struck out on his own. He had gone on taking those lives he chose to take in honorable duels. He always gave his opponents the chance to fight. He had been gratified at just how many had tried, gamely, to do just that. The survival instinct was truly powerful. It was more powerful than almost anyone realized, he concluded. He had seen it in action.

He knew that his duels were an attempt to recapture for himself that sense of survival spirit. In the face of inevitable, imminent death, fighting for his life in the short term simulated what he could not achieve in the long term. He grasped his own psychology well enough to know that much.

He knew Chamblis and his people hunted him. His phone, which he still carried with him, had not stopped ringing, although the frequency of the calls had dropped. He had promised himself that the next time Chamblis phoned him, he would take the call, if only for his amusement. Who knew? Perhaps he could persuade Chamblis to duel him. Nothing would make him happier. Perhaps it was time for the student to become the master before he died of the brain tumor slowly eating away his ability to think.

"Please," the banker said—at least Farnham thought of him as a banker, and so in his mind the man was dubbed such. "Please, I don't want this. I don't have anything against you."

"I don't have anything against you, either," Farnham said. "In fact, I'm trying to help you. Pick up the knife."

"But why?" the banker asked. "Why me?"

"Why *not* you?" Farnham asked. He drew the knife from his belt sheath. It had a long, curved blade, maybe eight inches overall. The handle was carved from fossil ivory in the likeness of a dragon. It was Patrick Farnham's most favorite blade, one that he carried every moment. He had used it to kill no less than a dozen people. He'd actually killed fourteen, but he did not count those; he had not used this knife for them.

Farnham moved in. He drew the knife through a complicated pattern drill, carving the air with it, scanning the parking garage with his peripheral vision to make sure they were not about to be interrupted. That happened, sometimes; sometimes *mundanes* blundered into the dueling area and the engagement had to be postponed. There were two men in Detroit, wandering around somewhere, who would never know how close they came to dying by Farnham's blade when interloping observers had prevented Farnham from executing the lesson he had hoped to teach. If there were any justice in the universe, Farnham would find those two men before he died. He remembered their faces. He had a very good memory.

The will to live finally outweighed the banker's fear. He snatched up the knife, holding it awkwardly.

"No, like a hammer," Farnham said. "Hold it like a hammer. Lock your wrist. Use your arm. Cut the air and then try to cut me. You can do it. I believe in you."

The banker did not understand, or did not want to. He did not change his grip. Instead, he lashed out, the knife barely held steady, frantically stabbing the space directly before him as if he would create a shield of his knife's point.

Farnham had to admit that was not a bad strategy, overall. There was a saying among well-trained fighters: no one wanted to fight a beginner. This was because beginners were completely and totally unpredictable. Without training, no one had taught them what was supposed to work and what was supposed to be a wildly bad idea. They would do stupid things, things that trained fighters would never even imagine because the trained fighter operated from a preconceived structure. Farnham, who sadly was forced to fight amateurs almost exclusively in his pursuit of the discipline of the blade, had seen more bizarre attempts by completely untrained opponents than did most fighters over their entire careers. This was yet another new one.

"You give me more challenge than I expected, friend," Farnham said. "I thank you for that, even as I accept the knowledge you are about to bring me."

The banker screamed. Farnham ignored that. He dodged a clumsy thrust and then drove forward, slashing and cutting, using the leverage of his blade to move his opponent's knife arm aside. Then he was in and deeply stabbing, shoving the banker out of the way with a deft push of his shoulder, hooking his knife in and under the rib cage from behind. The death rattle came soon, too soon, and suddenly the banker, the human being who had fought so hard to live, was dead at Patrick Farnham's feet.

Farnham reached down and picked up the disposable

knife. He dropped it into a nearby trash bin. He took out a handkerchief he carried for the purpose, wiped off his blade and threw the handkerchief in the trash, too. If the cops found it there—and they might—he supposed some clue might eventually lead them to Patrick Farnham. But he doubted that the authorities would find him anytime soon. Chamblis was worried about his club's discovery, but Farnham would not betray the man. It was not Chamblis's fault that he lacked vision, or that he did not possess the driving force that pushed Farnham to greater discovery.

No, Farnham would keep Chamblis's secret. If the duelists found him before the authorities did, he would either defeat them or die fighting. If the cops caught him, well, they might try him, even put him in prison, but that would only give Patrick Farnham a little more time to think, to understand. And while he would regret not having the chance to use his blades anymore, it was not as if he would have the time to rot in prison, as the phrase went.

His car was on the uppermost level. It would be a long walk to return to it. He went without hurry, whistling.

And then he heard sirens.

No. No, it was too soon. Too soon! There was too much to learn yet; he could not afford to be caught. He patted his waistband for the Heckler & Koch USP Compact he carried. It was there, its chunky weight reassuring and firm. The gun was not elegant as was the knife, but Farnham needed its power. He needed its reassurance.

The sirens were coming closer. He would have to get out of here. But he would never make the top level and his own car before the police came, and if they blocked him in the car as he tried to flee, he would be trapped in a glass-and-metal cage.

He reached the street level and kept walking. His phone began to vibrate in his pocket. Without thinking, he reached for it and opened it. The caller ID said it was Chamblis.

"Patrick?" Chamblis's voice was incredulous. "Is that you?"

"I'll have to call you back," Farnham said. He saw the unmarked police car approaching, saw the two men in it looking straight at him. He folded the phone, doing his best to walk toward the most congested part of the street. They had seen him emerge from the parking garage, without doubt—the very garage into which several marked cars were currently pulling. Damn it! He had to have missed a witness, or someone had to have come along while he was fighting the banker and he just didn't notice. Someone had seen him with the banker prior to the duel and called the police. It was the only explanation. How long had he stood there, alone in his thoughts, before the foolish man had picked up the offered blade? How long could the police have had to respond?

Had he ruined things for himself?

He had no choice. He had to get away.

He broke into a full sprint, running for life as he knew it.

10

"There," Davis said, pointing from the driver's seat. "The man with the phone. He's looking at us. He's thinking about it…there he goes!"

The man on the phone, who had a shaved head, was of average height and build and wore a black pair of horn-rimmed glasses, broke into a dead run. He was headed for the cluster of people at the mouth of a pedestrian plaza. There would be no way to take the car through there.

"Pull up and stop!" Bolan said. "Let's go!"

They ran for it, pushing past the curious onlookers as rapidly as possible. The running man bobbed and weaved among the other people.

Bolan and Davis gave chase. They ran through the crowd at the pedestrian plaza, past shops and temporary stalls. They charged through narrow alleys that widened and then shrank again. They dodged still more people and, once or twice, police cars with uniformed officers. Neither man dared involve the uniforms in the chase, for there was no telling who might help and who might interfere. If the running man was a person of interest who had information vital to the mission, putting a fatal bullet in him would be every bit as bad as losing him altogether.

Their quarry ducked into a head shop of some kind. Bolan and Davis hurried after. No sooner had Bolan cleared the threshold than a glass water pipe on the shelf next to him exploded. The rapport of the .45-caliber pistol was deafening in the enclosed space.

Bolan snapped the Beretta 93-R out of its shoulder holster and flicked the selector switch to single shot. He dropped to one knee as more slugs broke apart merchandise above and around him. He was showered with tiny fragments and pebbles of glass. Leveling the Beretta, he knew he had no choice since the gunfire would endanger innocents and he could not allow that. If he had a shot, he would take it, and end the threat for good.

The layout of the store provided too much cover and concealment. The man with the shaved head was moving farther away, knocking over shelves and hurling glassware at the pursuers as he went, but neither Davis nor Bolan could acquire a clear shot. The sound of a bell signaled a back door being opened, quickly. Bolan ran.

He hit the street behind the shop and immediately threw himself to the pavement. A trio of .45-caliber slugs burned the air overhead. Bolan rolled, extended the Beretta, and almost took a shot.

There was no target.

The running man was already around the corner of the building. Bolan pushed off and kept going. Davis came running out behind him and looked at the soldier for direction. He pointed toward where their target had gone.

"I'll circle around the other side!" Davis reported. He leaped a small fence separating the building from the one next to it and kept running. Bolan, for his part, continued forward.

"If he takes a hostage," Bolan said into his earbud transceiver, "we're going to have problems. Keep up the pressure. Don't give him a chance to think of it."

"I'm trying," Davis said, his breath coming in gasps as he ran at top speed.

Then Bolan thought he caught a glimpse of the man with the shaved head running into a Laundromat. He pushed the door open carefully.

An elderly woman saw the gun in his hand and gasped, trying to hide behind her laundry basket. Bolan waved her off. "Federal officer, ma'am," he said. "Did you see a man with no hair come running through here?"

The woman pointed, one hand over her mouth. She was pointing to the restroom at the rear.

Bolan approached the restroom. It was a unisex stall marked as such; there would be a single toilet past the locked door and most likely no windows. The runner was trapped. Bolan backed off, oriented himself at forty-five degrees to the door and leveled the Beretta.

"Come on out!" he ordered.

"Davis," he said more quietly. "I may have him cornered."

"Still…running," Davis came back. "I thought I saw him—"

"Don't shoot! I'm coming out!" came the response from beyond the door.

"There's a gun on you," Bolan told him. "Don't try anything."

The door opened slowly. The man who walked out was indeed bald and wearing glasses. He was also about seventy years old. "Please don't shoot me," he said quietly. "I may be old, but I think I've got a few years left."

Bolan immediately dropped the pistol. "I'm sorry, sir," he said. "Federal officer. I thought you were someone else." He turned to go.

"You get him, son," the old man called after. "Whoever he is, God bless you, you go get him!"

Bolan backtracked. "Davis," he said, "I came up empty. He must have gone the other way. Do you have him?"

"I keep seeing him," Davis said. "I'm…where am I?" The detective rattled off the street names when he came to the next intersection. "I'm headed north!"

"I'll meet you," Bolan said. Reading the signs as he went, he angled to intercept. He stowed the Beretta under his jacket. As it was, enough shots had been fired in this vicinity that another visit from the Detroit Police would be imminent if they weren't already in the area, looking for the same suspect. Sumner wasn't going to like what was happening down here, but it could not be helped. Bolan would simply remind him of Brognola's dire warnings and hope that was enough to calm the situation.

He sidestepped and took a very narrow passageway, not even an alley, that separated two three-story buildings. It was so close he had to turn sideways. It was also very dark, in the shadow of the two buildings. Bolan was effectively blind, stepping from sunlight into darkness.

The bullet almost took his head off.

His sixth sense for combat had his nerves firing even as he heard the shot that echoed impossibly loud in the brick crawl space. He dropped, whipping up the Desert Eagle and pressing forward with it, knowing that if he did not respond he would be gunned down. He could not see so much as the silhouette of the gunman at the opposite end of the alleyway, but he could not hesitate. The .44 Magnum handcannon bucked in his fist.

He took aim at the sides of the building near the end of the alleyway, the only targets he could reliably identify. The heavy rounds kicked up sharp fragments of brick, which could only be spraying Bolan's opponent. The soldier poured on the firepower, laying down a protective screen as he crouched. He counted his rounds as he did so. To fire the pistol dry would create a gap his enemy could exploit.

He heard footsteps and the opposing fire stopped. The bald gunman had to have turned and fled. Bolan threw himself from the mouth of the fatal funnel that was the crawl space, expecting to get tagged, but no shots came. He turned left, then right, and saw his prey running at full speed through a small, controlled parking area behind a bank. The next few moments slowed to a crawl as Mack Bolan's mind processed what he knew would be the fleeing shooter's next move.

A uniformed security guard, doubtless assigned to the lot to take money for parking and make sure cars were not parked illegally, stepped out of the phone-booth-size guard hut when he heard the gunman's rapid approach. The gunman tackled him, rolling him over, and Bolan tried to get off the shot. It was no good; the guard's back was to him, a human shield protecting the shooter from the soldier's bullets.

"Stop!" Bolan yelled, projecting from his diaphragm.

The gunman froze behind the guard. He was smart. He crouched behind the poor man—a senior citizen in a white-and-black polyester uniform—leaving almost no part of himself exposed. He was pressing a gun into the man's back, denying Bolan even the weapon as a target.

"Well, well," the gunman said. He had a lilting voice, almost a professional radio personality's timbre. There was a smile in his tone that Bolan could not see and did not need to identify visually. "That's quite a weapon you have there, Mr....?"

"Cooper," Bolan said. "Justice Department. Put down your weapon. You're not leaving here. Not alive."

"That sounds very final," the man said. "You aren't very polite. You haven't asked me my name."

Bolan did not move. The triangular muzzle of the Desert Eagle did not waver.

"Farnham," the man with the shaved head said loudly. "My name is Patrick Farnham. If you look me up, you'll find my apartment empty. I don't live there anymore."

"What's your game, Farnham?" Bolan demanded. He was preparing a shot. Farnham, as he talked, was moving slightly.

Periodically his shoulder would peek into view above the guard's, since Farnham was taller. Bolan had only to time the shot and take it. It would have to be precise. He had to make sure to hit Farnham squarely to make him turn, put him off balance, or he would trigger his own gun into the guard's back.

"I know you," Farnham said. "I know your kind. You're thinking about it. You might even be thinking of putting a bullet through him to get to me."

Bolan was thinking nothing of the kind. "And if I am?" he asked. Keeping Farnham talking would give him the opportunity he sought.

"Then you just might be doing me a favor. Catch me if you can, man. I've got nothing to lose and a lot to learn. You could teach me."

Farnham shifted. He was moving into range. Bolan's finger tightened on the trigger.

"Detroit Police!" Davis shouted. His voice echoed in Bolan's earbud.

Farnham reacted instantly, shoving the guard forward, extending his pistol and firing several rounds as fast as he could pull the trigger. The guard ran, fouling Bolan's shot, as he tried to get out of the way but instead blocked Bolan's line of fire. Davis was running at them from the side, having skirted the bank from the opposite flank. He returned fire with his Glock, hitting nothing but pavement.

Farnham was around the building faster than Bolan would have thought possible. He grabbed the staggering guard and set him down, gently; the man was not injured and looked more confused and frightened than anything.

"Go!" Bolan ordered. Davis pursued with him.

Farnham vaulted a chain-link fence, using the cover of the metal trash bins that seemed to be everywhere. He fired a few throwaway shots, but they came nowhere near Bolan or Davis.

Then he was gone.

Davis broke left and Bolan right. The two searched the area, finding plenty of escape routes in this congested neighborhood of shops and small apartments. They did not, however, find any trace of Farnham, nor did anyone they questioned remember seeing him. The man had faded into an environment he obviously knew well.

Bolan was not pleased.

"I'm sorry," Davis said. "Cooper, I'm sorry. I thought it was a stalemate."

Bolan looked at him. Davis seemed earnest; he seemed genuinely upset. The Executioner would never fault a man for doing what he thought best, even if he failed. That was the willingness to take action, the sense of truth to a personal code, that drove Bolan to fight as hard as he did.

What he could not rule out, however, was that Davis might be cooperating, even reluctantly, with the corrupt powers that were here in Detroit. The man might even have started off with all the honesty, character and promise that Bolan had identified in him, only to buckle to subsequent pressure.

So which was it? Was Davis a well-meaning, honest cop who had screwed up? Or had he intervened specifically to help Farnham escape?

And if he had, what did it mean?

Bolan concluded that he simply did not have enough information to decide yet. Davis would bear watching, carefully. Bolan was a very good judge of character, but he was not infallible. No man could be. He would wait and see.

"You did your best," he said finally. Davis nodded. They made the long walk back to their parked car, which was now surrounded by milling Detroit police officers in uniform. Bolan had to flash his identification and Davis had to do some fast talking before they were able to extract themselves.

"Sumner's going to have a fit," Davis said. "We just had a

running gun battle through one of the most population-dense areas of the city."

Bolan said nothing.

They entered the parking garage and followed their noses—and the flashing blue-and-red lights—to the lower level. The medical examiner was there already. The crime scene team was taping off a section of the ramp. A body lay in a pool of blood.

To Bolan it was only too familiar a scene, and a reminder that he had only until this evening before things went completely insane.

Davis's phone began to ring in his pocket. He put it to his ear, listened for a moment and then looked both interested and relieved.

"Thanks, Sandy," he said. "You're a lifesaver. Talk to you when I get back." He snapped the phone shut and looked expectantly at Bolan.

"What?" Bolan said.

"Byron Slovic," Davis said. He took the slip of paper from his pocket that contained his original list. Then he took the sheaf of printouts from his jacket and looked at them, comparing the two. "Yes. That's it."

"Explain."

"Cooper," Davis said, "I think we just caught a break."

11

The name circled on the heavily creased sheet of paper was "Byron Slovic." Davis explained, as the two traveled by car to Slovic's home address, that he had checked with a friend in Records—the attractive young lady Bolan remembered—in order to have the affected records more deeply examined. While his cursory check of the files indicated which data went with which identifier, it could not tell him what might have been *removed* from the data. There were, however, ways to check the backup files for these discrepancies, and someone in Records whom Davis trusted was the only option. That had been his lady friend.

The information was fortuitous, for they would have been dead in the water otherwise, relegated to checking the list person by person with no real inkling of whether they were getting closer to their goal. Farnham had dropped out of sight. They could not afford to wait for him to kill again. They had no idea what his next step might be, especially if there was a very real reason the man would behave erratically.

Farnham had been true to his word. They had looked up the man's DMV records and scored a positive identification. Bolan had also contacted the Farm with this data. The results of a deep computer check, however, weren't helpful. Farnham was almost literally nobody: he wasn't important enough to rate much in the way of files. He had no reliable job history, no assets, and nothing to tie him to a permanent address. The apartment listed with his driver's license records had been recently occupied but was currently vacant. Davis had called in a favor and had Detroit PD sweep the apartment. They found nothing.

Farnham's medical records had proved more interesting. A brief interview with his doctor had turned up a past history of brain cancer that had seemingly gone into remission. Once Bolan flashed his Justice Department credentials, the doctor hesitantly began to divulge more information. He said that Farnham had returned to see him a while ago, complaining of severe headaches. The doctor had given him the dreaded news that the tumor was back, and that perhaps it had never gone away. In response to Bolan's pressing he had admitted that, yes, such a tumor might affect a man so severely that he became disconnected from reality, to the extent that he committed serial murder. When the doctor had started asking what this was all about, Bolan had been forced to brush him off. He was not going to divulge more details than necessary to gain insight into the mission.

They had issued an urgent bulletin for Patrick Farnham. The man's identity was being released to all law-enforcement agencies in the area; television news stations were being informed that Farnham was an escaped patient from a drug rehabilitation facility, considered armed and very dangerous. If Farnham showed his face in public again, they might be able to reacquire him. His presence in proximity to the parking garage made him the primary suspect in the murders.

The sweep of the garage had, of course, revealed the body of a civilian. The man had been knifed to death; his family was being notified. It was the exact pattern of the previous killings.

Byron Slovic was the next step. He had forwarded this

identity, too, to the Farm. Price and her team had sent back a workup as files to Bolan's phone. It was unremarkable. Slovic had been an Information Technology specialist at a local industrial firm. Calls to that firm's Human Resources department had revealed that Slovic was not unusual in any way, at least as far as his former employer was concerned. He had a good record and had even been recognized previously for consistent attendance. He had no disciplinary actions on file. Web searches for Slovic had turned up no incriminating social networking pages. By all indicators he was simply a random civilian.

Except that he could not be. If someone with access to the Detroit Police Department's records had taken the time and the trouble to change the data relating to Slovic, there was something about the man that had to be worth hiding. Otherwise, why conceal him? He would have been just another name on the list of the dead.

As they drove, Davis had made several calls, trying to get as much preliminary information on Slovic as he could. He had no family ties that were incriminating on the surface. Bolan had suspected Mafia connections, for someone in the mix had employed Mafia assassins to eliminate Bolan and Davis before they could interfere. Slovic, however, had no such reported associations.

Presumably, the man's death had been investigated at the time. The names of the officers who had conducted that investigation were not in the report that Davis's blond helper had discovered, but she was asking around. She had promised to call when she learned, if she could, who had been responsible. It would be a good indicator of just who had changed the data, or exactly who the unseen editors were trying to protect.

Slovic lived alone in a small, rented house amid a cluster of similar dwellings, all of them owned by the same landlord. Davis had tried to contact the woman, to no avail. Bolan simply drove them to the address as the detective navigated. When they reached the doorway, they discovered that it was still sealed with crime scene tape. There was dust on the tape and some of it had broken free.

"Been a while," Davis said. "No family to come clean up after him. The landlord's probably waiting out the lease to avoid any legal hassles."

"Or someone paid to have the place left well enough alone," Bolan said.

The soldier removed the Sting dagger from his belt and used its razor-sharp edge to cut the tape sealing the door. He tried the knob, but the door was, unsurprisingly, locked.

"I can have a search warrant in—"

Bolan took a half step back and planted the sole of his combat boot against the door, breaking the jamb. The door swung open.

"Or that," Davis said.

They entered the home. Dust coated every surface. Slovic had died months earlier and no one had been here since. It was a two-bedroom affair, with a small dining area and open kitchen, a living room containing mismatched furniture and a filthy bathroom. There was a video gaming system connected to a large-screen television in the living room, a few books on shelves mounted to the walls and a Japanese sword in a scabbard on a stand sitting atop the highest of the shelves.

Bolan took immediate interest in the sword. He went to the shelves, gently took the blade off the shelf and removed it from its scabbard.

Davis whistled. "Is it valuable?"

"No," Bolan said. "Not at all. It's also not decorative. This is a functional, modern-manufacture carbon-steel sword blade. You can buy this for a couple of hundred dollars through the mail or in some knife shops."

"There was nothing in his file about being a student of… what would it be called? Samurai?"

"Iaido," Bolan said. "The art of drawing the sword. Keep looking." He placed the sword back in its scabbard and put it back in its place.

The larger of the two bedrooms held no furniture. Instead, the room was completely bare...except for the weapons on its walls.

"Davis," Bolan said. "In here."

"Wow," the detective said.

"Yeah."

There were a few martial-arts weapons on display, including small sickles, called *kama*, and some more exotic kung fu accessories. Most of the weapons mounted to Peg-Boards on the walls were knives, however. A hundred or more of them.

They were every size and description, but none of them was what Bolan would have thought to be a valuable collector's piece. No, these weapons were all functional. He took one off the wall and examined it. It had been hand-sharpened by the owner, judging from the scratches on the blade. He tested it against his thumbnail. It had been honed to a razor's edge and then some.

This was an arsenal.

It was no different from a gun safe, Bolan realized. These were not toys, nor were they items of ceremony. They were the functional tools of a man who preferred the blade as his weapon of choice. Certainly Bolan had known many men, good and bad, who had similar leanings. He himself carried fighting knives almost all the time, on virtually every mission he undertook. While Byron Slovic's proclivities might seem strange to some of his coworkers or his employer, or even to some of his friends, there were plenty of men and women who shared his enthusiasm. They attended trade shows and read magazines devoted to the collection and use of tools like these.

But Bolan was sure it had to mean something more than that, in Slovic's case.

A wooden cutting board had been hung on the only wall not covered in mounted knives. A bull's-eye target in red and white paint had been added to the board. Stuck in the target were throwing knives of a type Bolan recognized as a commercially available, licensed copy of blades from a popular action movie. He took one of them from the board and turned it over in his hand. It was, he thought, not weighted all that badly, gimmicky though it was.

"Cooper," Davis said, "what the hell is this?"

"Check the other bedroom," Bolan said. "Find a computer or a Rolodex or something. A phone. Anything he might have kept addresses or business cards in."

"On it," Davis said.

According to the files—the real files, uncovered by Davis's contact in the department—Slovic's body had been found dumped. The reasons for that were becoming clear.

Byron Slovic had been some kind of knife enthusiast. While that didn't make him a serial killer, or someone who associated with serial killers, it was more than coincidence. There was some connection here to the widespread knife killings in the city. But what was it? What was Slovic's involvement, apart from being a victim?

Live by the sword, die by the sword, Bolan thought. Could it be that simple?

In the closet of the bedroom, which was really a tiny training hall, Bolan found more bookshelves. On these were texts devoted to the use of swords and knives. The soldier pulled the string connected to the closet light, illuminating the small space.

The books were how-to titles on knife fighting, some of them bearing exactly those words in their names. Most of them came from the same publisher, a specialty house devoted to action titles. The books accumulated were considerable, some of them copyrighted in the 1970s. There were even a few classic titles on military combatives and the use of knives in battle, textbooks that Bolan himself had read and studied.

Slovic was no random civilian. Clearly he spent a great deal of his time engaged in the study of knives and the accumulation of them. And whoever was covering up the information trail that would lead to those responsible had tried to erase Byron Slovic from existence.

Davis returned. He held a black address book in his hands. "I found this," he said.

Bolan took it and began thumbing through it.

"There's one thing I don't understand," Davis said, examining the books on the closet shelves. "If somebody tried to hide Slovic, why didn't they remove all this?"

"For the same reason they did a sloppy job covering their tracks in the computer," Bolan said. "Somebody thought it wouldn't come to this. And had we been killed as they'd tried to arrange, it wouldn't have."

"You've got a point."

Bolan thumbed through the address book.

"Cooper," Davis said.

"Yeah."

"You think I let him go. You're wondering if I'm dirty again."

"You have a way of attacking these things head-on," Bolan said, looking up.

"Look," Davis said. "I understand. Clearly we're up against a lot. You don't know me. I could say the same about you. You're obviously some kind of government spook. Don't try to deny it. You aren't any Justice Department operative. You're some kind of covert service or special operations war fighter. I'm not stupid."

"No," Bolan said. "Obviously you aren't."

"I give you my word, Cooper," Davis said. "I did what I thought was best. I wanted to catch him. I want to end this."

"Then stop talking," Bolan said, allowing himself a tight grin, "and let me look at this."

Davis actually laughed. "All right, Agent Cooper. You have a deal."

The book contained dozens of names, most of them women. There were the usual entries for doctors and dentists. There were work contacts and lawyers, and even directions to Slovic's mother's house. A much older address for "Mom" had been crossed out; evidently Slovic's mother had moved. It was a reminder that, whatever he was, Slovic had been a real person, with family and friends who, no matter what Slovic might have been involved in, would grieve for him.

"Strange that an IT professional wouldn't have all that in a PDA or something," Davis commented.

"Not really. A lot of them have a streak of contrarian Luddite in them." He thought of Kurtzman, back at the Farm. The big man was a genius when it came to computers, but he, like most brilliant tech-heads, had plenty of idiosyncrasies. The industrial-strength coffee he brewed came to mind.

Then Bolan found it.

It was an address that simply read, "The studio." There were numbers connected to this, but no names. The address was the only unusual one in the book and, given the accoutrements in Slovic's home, it was the most likely place to go next.

Bolan took a moment to send a text message to the Farm using his secure satellite phone. He requested a special courier be dispatched to the liaison police department immediately. The Farm had assets in place nearby; it would not take long to fulfill his request.

Davis's phone rang again.

Bolan listened as the detective answered the call. It was Sandy, and she had found the information the pair wanted. Davis hung up, shaking his head.

"What?" Bolan asked.

"You probably had this figured out already," he said. "The detectives who covered this place after Slovic's death. They were assigned to report anything unusual. They didn't."

"Slate and Griffith," Bolan said. It was not a question.

"Slate and Griffith," Davis stated, nodding.

12

"Police," Davis announced. "Step aside."

Bolan, standing behind the detective, took in the space beyond the nervous-looking young man in gray sweats who had answered the door. It was well-appointed, and the rent in this well-trafficked retail neighborhood was not likely low. He could see the expensive, one-piece full-length mirror on the far wall. The burnished wood of the various kung fu practice dummies bespoke quality and age. There were bladed weapons mounted on the walls.

This was the right place. Bolan was sure of it.

Stony Man Farm reported that the address was a rental, the rent paid to a holding company that was well shielded. Kurtzman and his team were currently working to decrypt the electronic paper trail leading back to a real human being. Bolan glanced at the Marathon TSAR chronograph on his wrist. The evening news was not far away, and when it hit, if he had not resolved this mission, all hell would be cut loose in the streets of Detroit. Panic would grip the populace. Frightened citizens would turn on their neighbors. And somewhere, Patrick Farnham was still walking free, on the hunt.

Was that the common thread? Were Slovic and Farnham both students here?

"I'd like to see some identification," the young man at the door said. Davis started to reach for his badge, then stopped himself. He looked back at Bolan as if resigning himself and then stepped aside.

"I think," Davis said as Bolan stepped past him, "that my friend here, Agent Cooper, would like to see your identification, too." He flashed his badge, then, almost casually.

"Uh," the young man said. "Paul, Paul Menard."

"Do you teach at this school, Mr. Menard?" Davis asked.

"Oh, no." Menard shook his head quickly. "I'm a student."

Bolan walked up and down the studio floor. Davis was playing, without subtlety, a game of good-cop, bad-cop with Menard. Bolan thought there was no harm in going along, except that he would have to depart from the script. Bolan was no cop, after all. He was a soldier, and he would bring a soldier's sensibility to this confrontation.

"Let's step into the office, here," Davis suggested, pointing to the small office off the main entrance. There was a desk, a computer and a couple of antique-looking wooden filing cabinets inside. The walls were covered in diplomas and scrolls of varying kinds, some of them lettered in Japanese. As Davis herded Menard into the office, Bolan stopped to examine the ranking certificates in the main training hall.

Bolan stepped into the office behind Davis. The detective had seated Menard at the desk and was no leaning over it, looking at the computer screen.

"I don't understand what it is you're looking for, Officer," Menard said.

"Detective," Davis chided him. "I want to know what it is you teach here."

"We teach martial arts here," Menard said.

"No," Bolan cut in. "That's not an answer." He looked at his chronograph again. He could hear the numbers falling in his head. It was time to turn up the heat.

"Look, I don't know who you think you are—"

Bolan reached across the desk, past Davis and grabbed Menard by the neck hole of the man's sweatshirt. He jerked, yanking Menard out from behind the desk, dragging him into the training hall. Davis hurried after but said nothing to interfere.

"This Reginald Chamblis," Bolan said. "The man whose name is on all these ranking certificates." He pointed, sweeping the wall of framed documents. "Multiple arts, none of which seem to be advertised here. So which is it?"

"Look, we're a private school!" Menard protested. "I don't know what you think you're proving, but I want a lawyer!"

"You haven't been charged with anything," Bolan told him, "and I'm not a cop."

The student's eyes went wide. Bolan picked him up by the sweatshirt again and threw him into the center of the training hall. Menard picked himself up, looked left and right as if hoping for help from invisible allies, and struck a pose, his arms held in a fighting posture before his body.

"Think about it," Bolan said. "Think hard."

"Come on!" Menard said. "I'll teach you what it means to step into this hall with disrespect!"

"Cooper," Davis began.

Bolan chopped his arm down in the air, a dismissive gesture. Davis got the hint and stopped talking. The soldier never took his eyes off Menard. He dropped his canvas war bag from his shoulder to the floor and shrugged out of his jacket, letting it fall to the floor by his bag. At the sight of the machine pistol in Bolan's shoulder holster, Menard's eyes went wide.

It was a ridiculous, melodramatic gesture, Bolan knew. But he was making a point. And he had an audience. There was a video camera in the corner, near the ceiling, and its red LED was blinking. He had noticed it the moment they walked into the place. The camera was connected to a small wireless router mounted directly to the wall. Whatever the camera was seeing or was meant to see, it was broadcasting that signal somewhere. The soldier had made an effort not to present a full view of his face.

Bolan then slowly shrugged out of his shoulder holster, placing it and the weapon it carried on the jacket. When he drew the massive Desert Eagle from its Kydex holster, Menard took a step back, still maintaining his fighting stance. Bolan did not bother to scoff at him. Instead he calmly removed the double-edged Sting dagger from his waistband and added it to the pile.

The Executioner took a step forward.

"Come on!" Menard breathed. He was flushed and starting to sweat.

In Bolan's eyes, this so-called fight was over before it had begun. He did not believe in talking when there was physical force to be inflicted. This was not, however, a typical engagement. Menard was a potential source of information. He was also going to be an example. Bolan's strategy from the outset had been to so unsettle the enemy to the point that the forces behind the Detroit killings would expose themselves in their eagerness to terminate Bolan's interference. So far, thanks to corruption from within the local police department, that strategy had worked beautifully, more quickly and efficiently than even Bolan had imagined it would.

Whoever was watching the video feed, presumably this Chamblis or any other figures involved with the studio who were somehow connected to the knifings, would know that justice was coming for them.

"Patrick Farnham," Bolan said.

Menard tried to hide his flicker of recognition, but it betrayed him nonetheless. He went a shade paler, waiting with his arms before his body, his fingers extended and rigid. He did not want to fight. He wanted to posture and threaten with the act of fighting. He was not prepared to face someone like Bolan, whose opposition obviously unnerved the young man.

"So he was a student here," Bolan said.

"I don't know who that is," Menard stated.

"You do," Bolan said. He stepped in and, without raising his arms or telegraphing his movement before hand, swung his open hand through an arc as he torqued his hips. The powerful open-hand slap caught Menard across the ear and jaw on his left side as Bolan pulled it through the target. Menard hit the floor, hard.

"Patrick Farnham," Bolan said. "I want to know what went on here, what you train in, and I want to know who's involved and what they're involved with. You're going to tell me."

Menard threw his legs out, spun them and whipped his upper body back to his feet. It was a showy move that looked great in movies, but Bolan was not impressed. Menard tried to go on the offensive, stepping in with a roundhouse kick that came in high and fast.

Bolan stepped away slightly and brought his elbow down on Menard's thigh as the kick came in. The muscle spasmed and Menard howled. He collapsed to the floor again. The soldier, calculating the damage he would do and making sure not to cause any real injury, lightly kicked the fallen Menard in the face. The toe of Bolan's combat boot bloodied Menard's lip and spun him over onto his back.

When Bolan attempted to step over Menard to pin him there, helpless, the younger man reacted with fury. He had, Bolan reflected, probably been conditioned to avoid being mounted like that; it triggered his survival reflexes. Menard scrambled backward and put his back into a corner of the studio where, Bolan was satisfied to see, the camera in the corner would have an excellent view of him.

"You've got the wrong guy! I'm a college student! I don't know anything!"

"If that was true," Bolan said, taking a menacing step closer, "you wouldn't have been so quick to fight when the police came knocking." He jerked a thumb in Davis's direction.

"He has a point," Davis put in helpfully.

Menard was angling for the blades mounted to one wall. Bolan let him get there. The young man snatched a long knife, snapping the light wires holding it in place, and pointed the sharpened length of steel at his tormenter. "I'll kill you!" he gritted.

They always made those dire predictions, Bolan thought. But when they had to announce it like that, it was damned hard to take it seriously.

The blade came in, swinging and thrusting. Bolan was not in the mood. He waited for the blade to pass him in an arc, stepped in and used his forearm to bump Menard's knife arm out of the way. At his angle to Menard's shoulder, it was easy to grab the knife arm in an arm bar with his right hand on the guy's wrist and forearm. He twisted with his left arm, pushing against the back of Menard's shoulder, as he pulled with his right. His opponent screamed and dropped the knife. Bolan kicked it aside.

He spun Menard, balled his fist and punched the kid in the nose.

Menard bleated. His hands went right to his face as blood spurted from between his fingers. Helpless and completely disoriented, he bounced off the full-length mirror as he backed into it, then hit the floor, sobbing and squirting blood in equal measure. Bolan backed off a step. He had put on enough pressure. He took no pleasure in it, but Menard had been spoiling for a fight. The Executioner had simply obliged him. Finally the man might be softened up enough to answer some questions.

When he had waited long enough to see if Menard would collect himself and attack again, Bolan walked over and grabbed the back of the man's sweatshirt. He dragged the blubbering Menard out of the room and back to the little office, throwing him into the chair. There was a box of tissues on the desk. Bolan ripped out a wad of them and thrust it into Menard's face, taking the man's nearer hand and guiding it to his leaking nose. Menard held the tissues in place as they began to soak up blood. A wayward drop of crimson splattered the top of the desk.

"Patrick Farnham," Bolan said. Davis appeared in the doorway but kept his distance, giving the soldier time and room to work.

"He…was a student here," Menard admitted. "He left."

"Left how? Why?" Davis asked.

"I don't—"

"Skip it," Bolan cut in. "Student of what? I want an explanation." He shot a reproving look at Davis, who held up his hands as if to apologize.

"We learn the blade here," Menard said slowly. "The knife."

"And Chamblis?"

"He is the Maestro," Menard said. "The master of arms. He teaches us to wield the blade and to face it in honorable combat."

"Honorable combat?"

"We fight!" Menard said. Blood flecked his lips as he said the words. "We face the blade. We take life with it."

"You murder people," Bolan said.

"Only those no one will miss!" Menard insisted. "The worst of humanity. Bums. Drug addicts. Whores. We remove them. We experience the blade, and society benefits!"

"You cut up unarmed, helpless civilians," Bolan said.

"We don't!" Menard bleated. "We give them a chance. A knife of their own. A chance to fight back. It has to be mutual combat to mean anything. They want to live. They fight for it. Any of us could be killed doing it."

"So you're duelists," Bolan said.

Menard looked up. "Yes," he said. "It's what we do. It's what I live for."

"I want you to tell me everything you know about Reginald Chamblis," Bolan said. His phone began to vibrate in his pocket. He did not take his gaze from Menard's swollen face as he opened the phone and put it to his ear.

"Cooper," he said.

"I have an address for you," Barbara Price said. "Bear and his people tracked your studio to its ultimate owner. His name is—"

"Reginald Chamblis," Bolan interrupted.

"That's right," Price said. She did not sound surprised that Bolan was ahead of the game already. "I'm transmitting an address to your phone. It's Chamblis's estate outside Detroit. Bear and Akira did some digging."

Bolan nodded, though she couldn't know that. Akira Tokaido was one of the Farm's best hackers, a gifted cybernetics expert in his own right.

"Chamblis is connected to the Detroit underworld for starters," Price said. "He owns a controlling interest in a law firm that handles most of the defense work for the crime Families in the area. Some of the goons you took down were actually directly in his employ as private security in the past. Akira even traced Chamblis's credit cards. The guy has spent thousands of dollars on, get this, knives over the last several years. He pays top dollar to custom makers, among others. Ordinarily I'd say he's just a rich man who likes to collect knives, as some people do. But add the underworld connection and the Detroit murders and, well…"

"Yeah," Bolan said. "Paints a picture, doesn't it?"

"What's your next step?" Price asked. "The evening newscasts are coming up fast."

"I'm going to the source," Bolan said. "I'm going to put my hands on Chamblis. Once he's in custody we can interrogate him, find out who else he's been spending time with. I've got someone here who's going to tell me everything he knows about his fellow knife-fighting students. When he's done, Davis and I will take a drive out to Chamblis's place.

In the meantime, get Bear's people on the computer here. It's online. It's at the address you gave me."

"Akira's already ferreted out the IP address range that will get us in. For all I know he's inside sifting through it already."

"Good," Bolan said. "Might be nothing, but there could be something in the files to incriminate the other members of this…this *cult* of dueling fiends."

"Get them, Striker," Price said.

"Yeah." He hung up. "Okay, Menard," he said. "Time to sing. I want everything you've got."

Something changed in Menard's eyes. His expression turned feral. The shame of his betrayal of his fellow duelists had to have hit him. Bolan had seen that expression before. It was the look of a man who is ready to kill or die to redeem himself.

Menard's hand shot out, going for something under the desk. Bolan cursed under his breath. Of course, in a place like this, there would be a weapon mounted underneath. When Menard's hand reappeared clutching a small automatic pistol, Bolan went into action.

He folded one leg, dropping into a kick with the opposite leg that caught the lip of Menard's chair and started to spill him out of it. As Menard flailed, Bolan could see the gun starting to leave his grasp as if in slow motion.

The three shots that came next battered his eardrums with their successive concussions. He whipped his head around and saw Davis, his arms extended in a classic police shooting stance, his face determined behind the blocky, deadly silhouette of the Glock pistol the detective carried.

Menard hit the desktop, dead three times over. There was a hole in his chest, another in his neck and a third right between his eyes.

Bolan stared at Davis, who looked back, surprise in his eyes.

"Damn it," Davis said quietly.

13

Unraveling. It was all unraveling.

Reginald Chamblis sat behind his expansive, hand-carved desk in an office bigger than many people's apartments. A bank of large flat-screen televisions faced him. He held the multifunction remote in his hand, pressing the keys urgently, angrily, as if his discomfiture alone could will onto the screens something that would calm him. The sound was switched off on all of the units; the closed captioning was turned on. Mozart filled the room from high-fidelity speakers hidden in the walls of Chamblis's opulent private study.

Several of the screens bore the insipid local programming that preceded news reports. There were situation comedies, afternoon talk shows and children's programming. He had several cable news stations tuned in, but expected to see nothing there. The talk of horrors around the globe did not distract him from what was coming.

He had seen, only too well, what threatened him. What threatened his entire empire. What threatened to end the way of life to which he had become so accustomed.

On two of the screens, he saw different angles of Menard's encounter at Chamblis's studio. Menard was a good man, and an eager student of the discipline of the blade, but he was young and, thanks to his inexperience, reckless. He had tried, Chamblis knew, to uphold the honor of what he had been taught. But what young man of Menard's limited life experience could be expected to stand against...*that?*

Chamblis pressed the button to reverse the digital recording and then watched the sequence again. On the screen, the big man with the dark hair, in profile, nodded to one of the cameras. This Cooper, supposedly of the Justice Department—knew that every second of what he was about to do would be transmitted to other eyes. Somehow that knowledge made the big Justice man that much more fearsome.

Chamblis realized, then, that he had never truly felt fear. He had always conquered other challenges so easily. Even when facing the weapons of his attackers, on that night so long ago, he had never truly been terrified.

On the screen, the big man methodically, efficiently took Menard apart. There was a grace to his movements, a coiled lethality that reminded Chamblis of a panther stalking its prey. Cooper was accustomed, Chamblis understood, to being the most dangerous man in any room he occupied. It was obvious in his carriage, in his gait. Chamblis had thought he and his duelists the predators in a sick society, taking down the weak, the infirm, the diseased, so that society as a whole would be strong. But as predators, they were nothing compared to the menacing Cooper, who was only too aware of the power he held at his command.

The casual contempt with which Cooper beat Menard into submission was the key to understanding the man. There was no passion in Cooper's fluid movements. He was not angry. He was not even particularly agitated, despite engaging in a fight that would have had most men's systems shaking from the adrenaline dump. No, Cooper waded through Menard easily and without rancor, his every strike calculated. Even the humiliating way he had dragged Menard from the room—here, Chamblis hit a button to switch to the hidden camera feed from the studio's office—seemed deliberate.

Chamblis realized he was watching an expert interrogator at work, a man who understood how the human psyche was put together. Cooper saw Menard only as a potential point of data. He systematically stripped away Menard's defenses, faking a fight that Menard desperately wanted, because this offered him the best opportunity to defeat Menard. That defeat was not physical, first and foremost, but mental. Menard was beaten mentally.

As he watched the drama unfold in the office, however, Chamblis knew that it would end badly. Menard was a poor loser. In sparring duels undertaken to first blood in the studio, he had reacted badly to losing to Andreas. He had not gone so far as to disgrace himself by striking at Andreas from behind once the duel was concluded, but he had entertained the thought. Chamblis had read it in his face, in the posture of his body, in the tense way he had answered Chamblis's questions and then quickly departed.

There was a gun in a holster mounted underneath the desk. All of the students knew it was there; it was to be used if one of the offal of humanity, one of the wretched human beings the duelists used as their prey, came calling at the studio. It was a possibility, after all. Some homeless person or drug addict might see the duelists in action and then follow to the studio. Such eventualities used to be the only real concerns Chamblis had regarding discovery.

He had not counted on a man like Cooper of the Justice Department.

He pressed the intercom on his desk. A terse voice responded. "Yeah."

"Tell your men," Chamblis said, "that the targets are here, and to ready themselves to use deadly force. My security personnel are already on alert."

"You got it. My men were promised a bonus if there was a gunfight."

"You will of course be compensated."

Chamblis released the intercom. Miserable vultures. He had cultivated the relationship with Detroit's crime Families because he understood the usefulness of extralegal resources. Certainly all of his businesses, particularly the unionized ones, had benefited from the association. He did not feel anything about it, as long as it worked.

When his sources among the police had warned him that figures in Washington were sending an investigator to check on the killings his paid cops had worked to hide for him, he had hoped the firepower of the Mafia—inelegant a solution though it was—would end the threat. The overwhelming force he had employed was intended to send a message, too: Detroit is off-limits even to the highest authorities, so stay away unless you want a higher body count.

Cooper, whoever or whatever he was, had proved too resilient even for multiple Mob assassins. How the man, with only Detective Davis to support him, had managed to eliminate so many of the Mob killers, Chamblis had not been able to guess…until he saw the man in action at the studio. Finally he understood. Agent Cooper, whatever his real government agency might be, was obviously some kind of Special Forces headhunter. He was the most deadly killer Chamblis had ever seen, the very embodiment of the practiced lethality he had tried so hard to instill in the members of his dueling fellowship.

It galled Chamblis to again be relying on Mafia rabble to protect him, but he needed their backup more than ever. He would require what was practically an army to prevail—but he believed he had one at the ready. He owned a security company whose employees were selected for their willingness to bend the letter of the law to protect their owner. Most of them had criminal records; many of them had previous experience with weapons. Those who hadn't had it were given it as part of their training. The security firm, Red Falcon Protection, was essentially Chamblis's private army, a force ultimately loyal to him alone, well paid for its discretion and its fealty. Their crimson uniforms marked them as they stood at attention; a pair of them were outside the doors to his study. They would know how to respond. The Mob muscle he had contracted to bolster them, in anticipation of a need just like this one, was less disciplined, but they were vicious killers, all, and would be sufficient if any group of men could be.

There were certain less reliable persons with whom he needed to speak, however.

He picked up the ornate phone on his desk and dialed a number. It was answered on the first ring. "Griffith."

"Why are you trying to fuck me?" Chamblis roared without preamble.

"Sir?"

"You and your partner," Chamblis said, "have been well paid. So far you've given me nothing. And now the devil is at my doorstep! I thought I told you to get your asses over here!"

"We're on our way, Mr. Chamblis."

Chamblis looked up at the monitors covering the estate's surveillance system. A battered Crown Victoria had pulled up to the front gate. One of the men who exited the vehicle was unmistakably Agent Cooper.

"You should already be here!" Chamblis shouted. "You both have families, Detective. If you don't want your mothers, daughters and wives raped, your houses burned to the ground, and every finger of both hands broken, you will make sure Cooper and Davis don't leave these grounds alive!"

"Please, sir—"

Chamblis pressed the receiver hook. Damn them for fools. It would seem you just could not buy adequate police protection these days. Sighing, he dialed a second number. Andreas Garter answered. "Yes, Maestro," he said.

"Are you in position?"

"We are, Maestro. He has not appeared yet."

"He won't," Chamblis said. "Patrick won't be early. He will show up at exactly the appointed time. Nevertheless it was imperative that you and our people be in position ahead of time. You know what to do when I give you the signal." Farnham had always been punctual where the ceremony of the duel was concerned. Chamblis knew that the only way to corner the man, the only way to reel him in long enough to hook him, was to challenge Farnham to a duel. A duel with Chamblis was the thing Farnham desired most in the world. Chamblis could relate to Farnham's disturbed psyche well enough to know that much. Disturbed he might be, and without any sense of restraint, but Farnham was a duelist before anything else.

"Yes, Maestro," Garter said. "Forgive me, Maestro, but… it seems…"

"Beneath us?" Chamblis asked. "Yes, Andreas," he said. "I suppose it is. But Farnham is not one of us anymore. He is not entitled to the honors or the consideration that we would give one of our number. He is an aberration. A madman. A cancer, if you will. He must be cut out. You do not consider the tastes, the propriety, the sensibilities of a cancer before you remove it. You do not concern yourself with manners when a crazy man demands you face him."

"I understand this, Maestro. I simply mean… Well. You know best."

"Yes, I do," Chamblis said. "I will join you as quickly as possible. There is a problem here that I must resolve. In the meantime, I want you to call the airport. Have my plane prepared and fueled. Have the pilots placed on call. I pay them well enough to do nothing most of the time. They can sit in their plane and await us."

"Us, Maestro?"

"We have to leave the country, Andreas," Chamblis said. "If I cannot contain the threat, we must go. We will take those members of our fellowship as we can. Call the others and see to it they understand. If we cannot contain the exposure, if I cannot stop the Justice Department agent and his police department lapdog, the brothers and sisters of our fellowship will be in danger of discovery. When that happens, I will not be able to protect them here."

"But the Families," Andreas protested. "Surely they could intervene."

"The Mob has its influence here," Chamblis said. "But they have lost many…employees answering my calls. They were grudging in their response to this last need. If the men they have sent me are not sufficient, if their hired guns combined with my own private security officers cannot turn back the enemy, there will be nothing more they can do. They rely on shadows to accomplish what they do. To try to thwart the wheels of justice in broad daylight, with the public aware of their machinations…it would be too much to expect of them."

"But, Maestro, I have many of the security personnel here," Garter said. "Let me send them back to you. I do not need them all merely to safeguard us from one man."

"Do not underestimate Patrick," Chamblis said. "But I am hedging my bets, placing my pieces on this chessboard as best I may. I am dispatching one contingent of our Mafia assistance to you as well. I am about to place a call. It may come to pass that we will receive information from within the police department yet, and when that happens, I need you, or both of us, to have access to the manpower to continue working to eliminate our foes. You understand this?"

"I do, Maestro," Garter said. "Please, Maestro, the fellowship cannot survive your loss. I would give my own life if it were required, to see you to safety."

"I thank you for that, Andreas. But we will rebuild. And it may yet be possible to stop the threat, to hold it here."

"I will do as you ask, Maestro."

"Thank you, Andreas." Chamblis replaced the receiver gently in its cradle.

The building shook.

The sound of the explosion came to him, then. It was followed by another, and another. The rattle of automatic gunfire began to echo through the big house. The vibrations of a furious gun battle were transmitted through the marble floor to Chamblis's feet.

He took the elaborately engraved Korth revolver from his desk. There were speed loaders filled with .357 Magnum hollowpoint bullets as well. He took these and shoved them into the pockets of his tailored suit jacket. Then, as if it were an afterthought, he reached up, loosened the silk tie at his neck and yanked it off, throwing it into the wicker trash basket by his desk.

Chamblis burst from the study. "Come with me," he told the security guards. "We have a meeting to attend. We're getting out of here."

As they neared the juncture to the carport, the intensity of the gunfire increased. Chamblis heard men scream. He approached the door to the connecting corridor with caution, revolver in hand. His security guards flanked him. Each man had an illegal micro-Uzi in a shoulder harness. Access to hardware like that was one of the other reasons Chamblis had thought his Mob connections a worthwhile investment.

He opened the door a crack and peered out. Bodies littered the driveway. His perimeter guards, as well as the team of Mafia goons he had detailed to the front of the estate, had obviously been decimated. He saw only a few still moving. Two Mafia gunners and a trio of uniformed guards had taken cover behind a Range Rover in the carport. The Rover was now riddled with gunfire. Beyond it, Chamblis saw his Ferrari waiting, intact and ready. He had to reach it.

"How did they get so far?" one of the guards asked.

"It doesn't matter now," Chamblis said. He saw the big man, Cooper, pop up from cover behind one of the low walls delineating the estate drive. The oversized pistol in Cooper's hand barked, spitting what had to be two or three bullets in one burst. It wasn't a pistol at all, Chamblis realized, but some kind of miniature submachine gun. One, then another of the uniformed guards went down. The other men behind the Rover tried to make a break for it.

Chamblis had only precious moments to make this work. He shouted to his guards before they could figure out what was happening. "Now! Run! Cover me!"

They broke from the corridor and ran across the bloody battleground that was the carport. Chamblis made sure his uniformed guards were between him and his enemies. Withering gunfire rained down on them. Chamblis ran and did not look back. He heard the wet thumping sound of bullets piercing bodies behind him and to his left. He prayed he would not feel the burning, numbing sledgehammer of a piece of lead entering his own body.

Chamblis reached the Ferrari and threw the door open. The last of his guards went down before his eyes. He turned the key and the engine growled its throaty, exotic rhythm. He threw the car into gear and rammed the pedal to the floor.

Bullets tore into the windshield and the hood as the Ferrari rocketed from the carport and bounced over the outstretched legs of one of the fallen mafiosi. He shot past Cooper and Davis. Bullets sparked and pinged from the rear of the car, but none struck a tire. He was moving too fast; the Ferrari was a missile and he was riding it to escape.

As he put the estate behind him, he could not shake the feeling that he would never see it again. He vowed not to give in to despair.

He had an appointment to keep and a man to kill. That man was more than just an opponent to be defeated. He was an enemy to be smashed, a traitor to be punished.

His duel with Patrick Farnham was personal, and Farnham was going to die.

Chamblis shifted gears, urging the Ferrari to over a hundred miles per hour, desperate to put distance between himself and the men who sought the destruction of everything he knew.

14

"Look out!" Davis shouted.

The tomato-red Ferrari shot from the carport like a mobile weapon, its engine at the red line and its speed unbelievable. Bolan took several shots at it, snapping them off unaimed as he threw himself to the side. One of the thick tires left a smudge of rubber on the very tip of his combat boot; Chamblis had come *that* close to running him down. Bolan fired after the car, but the angle was bad and he was blocked by the twist of the driveway perimeter wall. He could not get a clean shot at any of the tires.

There was no point in mounting a pursuit. Chamblis had too great a lead and was moving too fast for Davis's borrowed Crown Victoria. They would need to return to the police station to regroup and collect Bolan's courier package. Once there they would determine the next step. The Farm had sent copious files on Chamblis. Bolan would review them and determine if there were any likely targets, locally. If the wealthy leader of the dueling cult tried to flee, as he most certainly would, he would leave a trail of some kind, a trail the Farm would help Bolan track. No matter where Chamblis went on the face of the Earth, no matter what name he assumed, the Executioner would find him.

But first things first.

Bolan pushed himself to his feet and swapped 20-round magazines in the Beretta 93-R. Davis looked a little shell-shocked, but he had handled himself well during the fire-fight to penetrate the estate. They were surrounded by dead gunmen. Bolan thought it safe to assume the men in street clothes were more Mafia-supplied guns, or just street muscle hired through whatever channels Chamblis had available to him. The uniformed security guards were from a company that was owned, ultimately, by Chamblis. This was verified in the Farm's data dump on the man.

Bolan's combat boots crunched over spent shell casings. He checked the nearest men to make sure there were no survivors. If they found anyone alive, Bolan would call for an ambulance. Davis was on the phone already, informing his lieutenant of the firestorm they had walked into on the grounds of Chamblis's home. From the look of it, Davis was doing a lot of listening and Sumner a lot of yelling. That was not a surprise.

Bolan saw movement and raised his gun again. A car was moving up the driveway. It was another Crown Victoria. Behind the wheel were two familiar faces.

Slate and Griffith.

The two detectives stopped their car and exited the vehicle. Griffith's finger was in a splint. Slate still had a bandage over his broken, bruised nose. Neither man looked happy. Their hands were very near the butts of their holstered guns.

"Well, well," Griffith said, sounding pleased. "Looks like it's up to us to bring you two mad vigilantes to heel. I'm afraid I'm going to have to ask you to put your weapons on the ground and come peacefully. You're both under arrest."

Bolan broke and ran.

Davis was apparently too stunned even to protest as Bolan grabbed him by the collar and dragged him along. The soldier ran back into the carport and pushed through the doorway to the connecting corridor, realizing as he did so that this had to have been the way Chamblis had come.

The estate had been well protected. He and Davis had been forced to fight hard to get as far as they had. Ultimately, however, the gunmen weren't up to the task. They had the will and they had the hardware, but they weren't experienced warriors. When the gunfire they had laid down was answered by Bolan's own firepower, augmented by Detective Davis's fire, they had fought with poor coordination. Bolan had used that disarray to his advantage, moving among them and chopping them apart piece by piece.

"Where are we going?" Davis asked.

"Combat stretch," Bolan said. "We need room to operate." He picked the first left turn off the corridor and continued on, still towing Davis with him. Behind them, gunshots sounded. The crooked detectives were shooting at them as they pursued.

"Now might be a good time to rethink your policy on shooting cops," Davis said. Bolan had no response to that.

They crossed a pair of rooms, Bolan doing his best to leave furniture and other obstacles in the dirty cops' way. He tore through the house, kicking down any door that did not immediately open. Davis covered them from the rear, glancing back nervously. Several times they heard more shots, and the shots were closer. Despite Bolan's best efforts, Slate and Griffith were gaining.

They found themselves in an expansive kitchen. Bolan pushed Davis to one side, out of the line of sight from the door, and flattened himself against the other side of the opening, next to a large stainless-steel refrigerator.

It was Griffith who was first through the doorway, hurrying with a larger revolver in his fist. Bolan wrenched open the refrigerator door and threw it against Griffith with all the force he could muster. Griffith actually bounced, rebounding from the door and leaving a large dent in it. He hit the corner of the steel table island in the center of the room, groaned and hit the floor like a sack of wet grain.

Slate was smarter. He saw what happened to Griffith and hung back, emptying his gun through the doorway. Bolan was driven back. Where he had stood a fraction of a second before, Slate's rounds punched holes in the air. The supersonic crack of the man's issue-approved Glock was answered by Davis's own as the detectives exchanged fire.

"He'll call for backup and then all bets are off," Davis shouted. "They may already have reported us."

"We'll deal with that when it comes," Bolan warned. He reached into his war bag and pulled out a fragmentation grenade. "Get ready," he said.

More bullets were followed by a lull and the sound of Slate reloading. Davis put his hands over his ears and squeezed his eyes shut. He was braced for an earsplitting explosion.

Bolan wound up and chucked the grenade like a major league pitcher. The heavy bomb, a metal sphere slightly smaller than a baseball, hit Slate in the center of his face. The detective's head snapped back as he screamed in pain. Bolan had hit him in his broken nose.

The grenade, its pin and spoon still in place, bounced harmlessly across the floor.

Bolan came through the door fast. He snatched up the grenade to make sure it wasn't used against him, dropping it back into his war bag as he went. Slate was holding his face and writhing on his knees, the pain in his face too much for him.

Bolan closed in on the bent cop and felt his blood begin to boil. This man had been responsible for countless deaths, either indirectly or by covering up the work of the duelists so they could continue their crimes. When Slate's head came up and something like awareness returned to his eyes, Bolan kicked him in the throat. Slate hit the floor flat on his back, scratching at his neck and making choking noises.

"Keep an eye on him," Bolan said. He turned to go back into the kitchen.

Slate wasn't out.

His Glock was on the floor, but the backup weapon came from nowhere. It was a tiny North American Arms Mini-Revolver. The fallen detective, still choking, extended the diminutive pistol and cocked back the hammer. From the length of the gun, it was a .22 Magnum. Bolan had time to shift his weight, preparing to leap. He would have to time his evasion just right, during the window of opportunity when Slate's hand and arm tensed prior to the shot.

Davis shot the detective in the face.

Slate was dead before gravity was done with him. He hit the floor wetly.

Davis looked at Bolan—the soldier said nothing, but he offered the detective a nod as he stepped back into the kitchen.

Once there, Bolan grabbed Griffith by the lapels of his coat. With one furious heave he dumped the detective on the stainless-steel table, grabbed a large butcher knife from the wooden block nearby and put the huge triangular blade under the detective's neck.

"Do you know how to carve a turkey, Griffith?" Bolan asked. "Your Mafia buddies, they know all about it."

"They're not my buddies," Griffith protested. "I don't deal with the Mob. That was Chamblis. Chamblis! He did it!"

Bolan went on as if he hadn't heard. "You wouldn't believe the things I've seen," he said, using the knife to cut open the front of Griffith's shirt. Buttons popped and hit the floor. "Men and women reduced to lumps of suffering meat. People with their faces just…gone. Every extremity you can imagine severed and dumped. When the Mob interrogators and surgeons got done with them, they weren't anything recognizable as human anymore."

"Don't! Oh, God, don't! I'll tell you anything you want to know!"

"You know about the duelists," Bolan said. "Spill it, or I'll spill your guts out on this floor."

"We got word the usual way," Griffith blubbered. "Through snitches, street informers, that kind of thing. There was a major player on the block, somebody new, somebody well connected looking to set up shop in Detroit."

"Chamblis."

"Yeah," Griffith said. "He asked around, discreet like, the way you do. Didn't want to say too much. It was Slate who brought me in, told me what was what. I don't know how Slate hooked up with him at first. I didn't ask."

Bolan doubted Griffith was as free of original sin as he tried to claim, but that wasn't his concern. The detective was talking and filling in holes. "Keep going," he prodded, pressing with the knife.

"Okay, okay, please, don't frigging cut me with that thing," Griffith pleaded. "We got a call. Every time a body was going to show up, they let us know ahead of time. The bodies were nobodies, street trash. Nobody was gonna care one way or another. Probably would have offed each other eventually without help, the lives they led out there. What difference did it make? He was paying us so much money. We did what we could."

"You helped him cover up the murders as they occurred," Bolan interpreted. "You altered the computer records, too, knowing that eventually someone might come investigating."

"Yeah," Griffith said. His eyes went to Davis, who was watching from the doorway. "Figures it would be that little wet-nose bastard. Little Boy Scout. Never knew when to lay off when it was none of his business—"

"Shut up," Bolan said. "When I want your editorial opinion, I'll shoot you in the kneecap for it. The rest. Now."

"We didn't know what it was about," Griffith said. "We figured, take the money, who was really being hurt? But then the department got word that Washington was sending a Fed to investigate. You. So we poked around, got what we could and let Chamblis know."

"Because you knew he'd pay you extra for the information," Bolan guessed.

"Well, yeah," Griffith said.

"So Chamblis paid the Mob to assassinate us both," Bolan said. "Get us out of the way to keep a lid on his dueling cult."

"Yeah," Griffith said.

"Which doesn't explain how they found us, or knew when to hit us."

"We've been tailing you," Griffith said. "It wasn't so easy when you were driving, but Davis, he's a rookie."

Davis bristled at that. Bolan waved a hand. "You were following us and reporting our location?"

"Yeah," Griffith said. He sounded close to tears. "You gotta understand, man, that guy is insane. We figured when the money was coming in that it wasn't worth checking out, but he's been getting more and more demanding. Calling us. Threatening us. Threatening our families, man!"

"The victims of Chamblis and his monsters had families," Bolan said.

"But don't you see, man," Griffith said. "For years this went on. For years they never took out anybody who raised any flags. They could have kept right on doing it. But something went wrong. They started killing people just pulled off the street for walking down it, or something. I think Chamblis was losing control of his crazies, losing his grip."

"Explain."

"He was on us day and night to keep a lid on it, and to help him take you out," Griffith said. "Like the people getting killed, the people bringing all the heat, weren't his choice. He was really pissed about it, man."

"Did he ever mention a Patrick Farnham?" Bolan asked.

"Farnham, no," Griffith said. "But he let slip the name Patrick. He wasn't happy about it. He was canvassing the city, had his freaks out looking for this guy. I think he was a member of their group. Slate thought it was this guy Patrick doing these new killings, the really obvious ones. That was his theory. Poor, dead bastard."

Bolan removed the knife. Griffith breathed a sigh of relief.

The Executioner turned to Detective Davis. "He's all yours."

"Nothing would give me more pleasure," Davis said, "than to put the cuffs on this guy."

Griffith was weeping when Davis pulled him down from the table, dusted him off and read him his rights. The younger detective seemed, indeed, to be taking great pleasure from the act. As the cuffs went on—Davis's department-issue tempered steel cuffs, not one of Bolan's zip ties—the disgraced cop hung his head.

It did not take long for more police to show up. Davis, once more to his credit, took immediate charge. The gunfire that had brought a police response had the officers on high alert, but Davis showed them his credentials as Bolan waved his Justice identification around. Davis also made sure that appropriate bulletins had been issued for Chamblis. Then it was time to see Griffith packed into the back of a squad car.

"What's going to happen to him, Cooper?" Davis said as the car drove away. Griffith stared out the rear window, looking lost.

"He'll face justice," Bolan said, as the two men walked among the dead and the carnage to the beaten-up Crown Victoria that had served them so well to that point.

As Davis climbed in behind the steering wheel, he looked thoughtful.

"Now what?"

"Until we get a lead on the whereabouts of Chamblis or Farnham, we don't have a next move," Bolan said. "We also have no more time." He looked at his watch.

"So what does that mean? We've lost?"

"Hardly," Bolan said. "It's at times like these, when it gets quiet, that prey you've backed into a corner comes after you, snarling. We won't have to find Chamblis or Farnham. One of them will make themselves known, somehow. That's how desperation, a product of external pressure, works."

"You planned all this," Davis accused. "Everything you've done has been to put pressure on them, bring them out of hiding, so you can identify the bad guys and then take them out."

Bolan said nothing.

"Back to the station, then?"

"Yeah," Bolan said. "I'm expecting some mail."

As they drove, Davis looked over the bodies one last time. They exited the estate and the detective pointed them in the right direction. "What makes a man turn dirty, Cooper?"

"The fact that you don't know the answer," Bolan said, "is probably why you haven't done it."

"Yeah," Davis said.

15

The abused engine of the bullet-pocked Ferrari ticked as it cooled. The car was tucked away in the lowest level of the parking garage, immediately below them. This garage, the scene of one of Farnham's previous crimes, was ideal precisely because the cops had already combed through it. There was still police tape here and there, and evidence of the countless minions of law enforcement having wandered through the place.

The thought made Chamblis sick. Thanks to the police, thanks to the sinister Agent Cooper, thanks to the failure of both his contacts within the Mafia underworld and among his own resources, he was going to have to disappear. Everything he had built, everything of which he was proud, would have to be left behind. He would need to change his identity. He would have to travel to a country where he could not be extradited. There would be no other way.

He was damned, however, if he was going to leave Detroit without first seeing to the end of the man who had caused all this. He had challenged Patrick Farnham to a duel, and he was going to take great pleasure in seeing to it that Farnham's miserable life was snuffed out.

He had a large force of his own security officers and hired

Mafia enforcers backing him up. They would be more than adequate to the task of taking out Farnham. Would they be enough should Agent Cooper descend upon him again? He wasn't sure. He hated this, hated being on the defensive.

A man who fought a defensive duel was doomed. An enemy who had the initiative could move in on you at will, dictating the terms of the fight. He would whittle away at your defenses, carving you up, waiting for fatigue, blood loss, or cumulative injury to reduce your abilities until he could end your life. It was a dishonorable way to lose a duel. Far better to go out while at full strength, striking and being struck, feeling at once the shock and surprise of an enemy's steel in your gut. Your life would leak out and then it would all be over, and you would finally know true enlightenment....

He was broken from his reverie by a report from Andreas Garter. Garter had insisted on staying with him and seeing this through. The man had true loyalty. The other members of the fellowship of the blade were presently at the airport, waiting to take off on Chamblis's private jet. He might have lost everything here, he told himself, but he could easily use his skills and his knowledge to build up new business interests elsewhere. With his brothers and sisters of the blade to support him, there was nothing he could not do. He would create a new studio, wherever they ended up. He would continue to train. He would reward their loyalty and faithfulness, too, with money he had hoarded in Swiss bank accounts. Garter, who had proved so reliable, would be the first to benefit. He would receive the greatest largesse. It made Chamblis proud just to look at the man.

Garter cut a fine figure in his closely cropped blond hair and crimson jacket. He had adopted the uniform of Chamblis's private security in order to reinforce his authority over them. Chamblis had personally placed the men at Garter's disposal. Garter, who had gained his military experience while a young man in West Germany, was fully capable of directing Chamblis's forces. The hysteria, the concern, the desperation of the last hours seemed to melt away while Chamblis was in the company of his men. He was regaining control. He was repairing, even controlling, the situation. Agent Cooper would not be able to find him here. Wherever the man was, damn his eyes, Chamblis would see to it the implacable golem was hunted and killed.

They would retreat to South America. Perhaps Argentina, Chamblis pondered. Garter had said he had visited Argentina and found it a pleasant enough nation, with opportunities for a man who knew business. Yes. That just might work. He would look into it.

His men were hidden among the columns and parked cars as best as they could be, though there was little enough real concealment here. But it would be enough. Farnham, in his madness and arrogance, would have no idea what he faced here.

"Hello, Maestro."

The words startled Chamblis, who stood, ostensibly alone, in the center of the level. Farnham stepped out of the shadows. He looked just as Chamblis remembered him; there was nothing overt in his appearance to suggest the insanity that lurked within.

"Patrick," Chamblis said. "You know what I must do."

"I know that you have challenged me to honorable combat," Farnham said. "And I have accepted your challenge."

"Why did you do it, Patrick?" Chamblis could not help but ask. "Why did you ruin us? Why did you disobey me, expose us as you have? You've ruined everything."

"I have ruined nothing," Farnham said. "You would have been content never to go further, never to know the true enlightenment of fighting a human being who is vibrantly *alive*. Under you, the fellowship would never have evolved."

"It doesn't need to evolve," Chamblis said. "It needs to be kept safe. Protected. You've destroyed that."

"It doesn't matter," Farnham said. "I haven't long, you know. I can feel that. The closeness of it has brought me clarity."

"You are insane."

"Do you believe you are not?" Farnham laughed. The lilting mockery left his tone and he sounded, suddenly, tired and sober. "You murder other human beings," Farnham said. "As do I. You have my madness. You just don't want to believe it."

"Enough," Chamblis said.

"I agree," Farnham said. He drew first one, then two knives, holding the blades aloft in a cross pattern before striking a pose with them. The points glittered under the overhead light. Chamblis, standing in the center of that light's underpowered cone of illumination, smiled.

"I don't think so, Patrick," he said. He raised his hand and chopped the air with it.

Men in red uniforms, led by Garter, stepped from hiding. They were joined by the more slovenly but no less fearsome Mafia hit men. They formed an arc before Farnham, the barrels of their automatic weapons trained on him.

"No," Farnham said. He dropped his knives. The metal rang on the pavement. "No, not like this. Please, Maestro." His voice rose in pitch, becoming a shriek. *"Not like this!"*

It was Garter who fired first. The other men joined him. The cacophony of their weapons accompanied a wave of warm air as the shock and discharge from the blasts rolled over Chamblis. He exulted in the power of that shock wave, despite the battering his ears took. In truth, he barely heard it so much as he *felt* it. It was the sensation of victory, of revenge enacted. He raised his arms as if conducting a symphony.

Bullets tore into Farnham, jerking him like a rag doll. He danced for what seemed like endless minutes, the look of horror on his face never once leaving it. Before it was over, Farnham was so much shredded meat, lying in a heap on the bloody pavement of the parking garage.

Chamblis breathed a sigh of relief.

The mad dog was no more.

Garter, reloading his Uzi, came to stand next to him, admiring the mutilated corpse of Farnham.

"His arrogance killed him," Garter said. "He died in shame, disgraced. It is good. You have done well, Maestro."

"Perhaps," Chamblis said. "But in truth, while I feel satisfaction in it, it brings me no happiness."

"And now, Maestro?"

"See to it that the Mafia jackals are paid well to ensure their silence," Chamblis said. "We will go to the airport. We must leave and begin to rebuild."

"There is yet time," Garter said. "We might still be able to stop the investigation."

"Do you think I can hold them together long enough to mount another attack?" Chamblis swept the assembled men with his arm. They were reloading and seeing to their firearms, paying Garter and Chamblis no real attention. It would be necessary to leave this place soon, for the gunfire would prompt calls, even at this depth in the garage. Someone was bound to have overheard and called the hated police.

"I believe in you, Maestro," Garter said.

"I am glad, my friend," Chamblis said. "But we do not know where Cooper and Davis are now. We don't know what information they might have transmitted, what evidence they have. We must assume that we will be exposed in any event."

"Then for revenge, Maestro," Garter said. "We kill them for the sake of our honor!"

"We have so little time," Chamblis said. "It would have to be immediately, if we are still to escape."

Chamblis's wireless phone began to ring. He glanced at

it and was going to ignore it until he saw the caller ID. He snapped open the phone.

"It is the police department," he said quietly to Garter with his hand over the receiver. Taking his hand away, he said, "Yes?"

"It's Bill Griffith," the voice answered him over the sound of heavy breathing. "Listen, man, I gotta say this and I gotta say it quick. This is going to be my only opportunity to call you."

"What do *you* want?" he demanded.

"I'm in custody," Griffith said. "I need your help."

Chamblis nearly hung up the phone in terror. He forced himself not to do that; he needed to know what Griffith offered him. The detective was not stupid enough to believe Chamblis would help him out of the goodness of his heart, and clearly the man hoped Chamblis's wealth and power would be enough to improve the fallen cop's lot.

"I am not in a position to help anyone," Chamblis said.

"Hear me out, man!" Griffith said. "I know if I was you I'd be pretty pissed. I'd be looking for some payback. You interested in some payback, man?"

"What," Chamblis said, his eyes narrowing, "will it cost me?"

"Your law firm," Griffith said. "I need you to assign somebody to me. A real shark. Somebody who can help cut me a deal for my testimony."

"You want me to help you save yourself at my expense," Chamblis said flatly.

"You're boned anyway, man," Griffith said. "You got to know that as well as I do. But I got one thing that can help you. I can help you get even."

"Spit it out."

"Cooper and his butt-boy, Davis, are here at the station now," Griffith said. The detective rattled off the address from long memory. "You want 'em, they're yours. Stake the place out and take 'em when they leave. They can't stay forever. You gotta move. We have a deal?"

Chamblis almost laughed out loud. "No, Detective Griffith," he said into the phone, "we most certainly do not have a deal. I hope you go to prison," he continued in a low voice, "and I hope the men you helped put there make you feel as welcome in your new home as you have made me feel in my old one."

"No, wait—"

Chamblis snapped the phone shut.

"Get the trucks," Chamblis told Garter.

"Maestro?"

"Revenge," Chamblis sent simply. "Tell me. Did you bring the item I asked you to get?"

"Yes, Maestro," Garter said eagerly. "Yes!" From within his jacket he produced a grenade. "Very powerful," he said. "Use it only if you must, Maestro, for it is very dangerous."

"I understand," Chamblis said. "One always needs an extra edge. Let us go."

They had traveled to the parking garage in a trio of white panel vans bearing the subdued red logo of Chamblis's security company. Chamblis promised the Mafia parasites a bonus if they accompanied him on this "hit," and they readily agreed. Their spirits were flying high, as only those of men accustomed to shooting unarmed, helpless victims can be. It took so little effort to pull a trigger, especially when your enemy had no hope of fighting back. Such men would never know the enlightenment of the blade. Chamblis was already, in his head, looking forward to establishing his new school in a new city. A change of scenery, far from the legal problems that would await him in the United States, was in order. He was persuading himself that it was a good thing, a positive thing. He would at least find, in the effort of reestablishing himself, enough to interest him.

The smile came to him unbidden.

He and Garter took the first van, his security guards piled in behind him. The Mafia hit men took the second and third vehicles. They would travel in caravan to the police station. They would wait until they saw Cooper and Davis exit the building, just as the idiot Griffith had suggested. Then they would kill both men before leaving this place far behind.

Chamblis had to admit that he would find it difficult to sleep at night, knowing that somewhere, Agent Cooper was alive. To picture that man stalking him, hunting him…he did not think he could live with that, not for long. Better to end it here. Better to know that he had driven a stake through the heart of this particular monster.

THEY ARRIVED after a relatively brief drive across the city. Chamblis directed his men to park on opposite sides of the road, with one van covering each of the possible approaches by car. It was imperative that Cooper and Davis not slip by them. They would have only this opportunity and no more.

The waiting nearly killed him. Chamblis had never been a patient man, as such. He was not given to quiet contemplation; he needed stimuli, needed problems to solve. Simply sitting and waiting in a van full of armed men was not sufficient to stop his mind from racing.

He had murdered Cooper and Davis in his mind a thousand times over before the two men finally appeared. He was not certain he was seeing it until he did. But there was no mistaking the big man who walked boldly from the front entrance to the station, down the steps outside. Davis, the detective, was with him.

Even doing nothing more dangerous than walking to his car, the man radiated danger. Chamblis could see in this Cooper the carriage of a fighter, to the man's very core. It was disturbing. The only other man Chamblis regarded so was himself.

Well. It was time to take the first step toward the rest of his life.

He signaled Garter, who took up his walkie-talkie and put it before his mouth. "Trucks two and three," he said. "Begin to move. Go slowly. Do not tip them."

The Crown Victoria, parked in a reserved space before the station, pulled away from the curb. Garter put the van in gear and followed. The other vehicles were already in motion.

"Truck three," Garter said. "Hang back. Truck two, you will be our spear."

"Understood," the voice of the security guard driving the second van said. Chamblis thought he overheard the man's Mafia cargo grumbling in the background. They just might, perhaps, understand what Chamblis had in mind. Well. They would get over it.

"Now," Chamblis said.

16

The police station receded in the rearview mirror as Davis turned the corner. Bolan's parcel was in the trunk; the Stony Man Farm courier had not failed him. Davis had suggested that Bolan take the opportunity to get some rest. He was driving the soldier to the hotel he hadn't yet had a chance to check into, where the soldier could get some sleep, a shower, or both while Davis returned to the department to monitor police surveillance and readiness channels. When something broke, Davis had promised, they could immediately respond to it. Bolan, who had been on the move without sleep more or less straight off the plane to Detroit, saw the wisdom in taking downtime when there were no other options.

Bolan looked out his window.

The white panel van struck the Ford with bone-crushing force. Safety glass disintegrated into a shower of rock-hard pebbles. The Ford spun in a 180 degree arc, coming to rest against the curb, its flank crushed and its rear driver's-side wheel flattened.

Gunmen boiled from the van, like angry hornets pouring from a nest. Some wore security guard uniforms, while others wore street clothes. They were approaching the pas-

senger side of the car when the door flew open and an aveng-
ing Bolan fired into their midst.

The Executioner charged from the car with a gun in each
hand. The .44 Magnum Desert Eagle roared; the Beretta 93-R
coughed its deadly triple-rhythm. Shells hit the pavement. In
a heartbeat, the men closest to the Ford fell to the pavement.

Bolan knew that to survive against overwhelming odds
like these required movement. He stayed in a crouch and
glide-stepped around the corner of the van, shooting as he
went. He shot a man in the face, got another in the neck. And
still another, partially concealed by the van, he dropped and
shot in the kneecap. When the gunman screamed and fell
from behind the vehicle, Bolan drilled him through the heart
with a single .44 Magnum round.

The Executioner was willing to run the risk of seeking the
high ground, for above the fray he would have a great field
of fire but also make a tempting target. Holstering the Desert
Eagle, he grabbed the mirror extending from the rear corner
of the van on an A-strut. Using this, he pulled himself to the
roof of the van, then flatted himself against it.

The gunmen shooting at him would have his range in only
seconds. He drew his Desert Eagle once more, extended his
arms as if he thought he could fly and began shooting from
the roof of the van. The fusillade pinned the gunmen nearest
to the van, striking and wounding some of them, killing still
others.

Bolan saw Chamblis moving among a knot of men farther
down the street. There were more assassins than the soldier
had realized. Apparently Reginald Chamblis himself was
leading the charge; it was most likely a last-ditch revenge
play, for Chamblis's public identity was blown here in Detroit. He would not be able to return to the country, much
less the city, if he managed to get away, but obviously he had
something besides escape on his mind in mounting this assault.

Bolan felt the van shake beneath him. There were men climbing back inside. They would try to shoot him through the roof.

He beat them to it. Holstering the Beretta and swapping magazines in the Desert Eagle, he held the triangular snout of the handcannon above the roof of the van and started pulling the trigger, walking the shots in an ever-wider pattern. Men screamed below him. Bodies hit the floor of the cargo van.

Civilian traffic had stopped on this part of the street. The drivers of the nearest cars had fled their vehicles, leaving them where they idled. These formed an effective roadblock, stopping other civilians from blundering into the firefight. Any pedestrians on the street had fled. Bolan was grateful there were no innocents caught in the cross fire.

Chamblis was sending a wave of reinforcements. Bolan flattened himself again and spun, shooting left and right, taking running gunmen this way and that. Bullets sparked and ricocheted from the corner of the van's roof.

It was time to move. He could not let them bracket him and then take shots at will. Shoving off with his hands, he dropped behind the van, careful to avoid bullets from below should anyone be trying for a belly shot while crouching beneath the vehicle. His combat boots kicked empty brass and left bloody footprints on the asphalt.

He took up a position behind the engine block of the Ford. He could not, at first, identify Davis's position. He finally saw that the detective had been forced into a corner at the stairs leading to a nearby building. The stone facade of the structure proclaimed it a multistory retail and office space; there were signs advertising vacancy and availability.

Davis was outgunned. He was taking automatic weapons fire and had been reduced simply to hunkering down and riding out the storm. Bolan took a two-handed grip on the Desert Eagle. From his flanking position he had a great shot at the gunmen, who were not aware of him for the moment.

He fired. The .44 Magnum hollowpoint round splattered the brains of one of the lead shooters, causing the others to look around for the forgotten threat. Bolan shot a second man and a third. The gunmen then focused on him again and he backed down behind the Ford, feeling the vehicle vibrate as it absorbed multiple rounds. He was careful to keep the engine block between him and the enemy.

Bolan surged from cover again, running across the street, drawing fire as he sprinted. He was trying to reach Davis, help shoot the detective out of the mess he was in. Together they could focus their fire, drive a wedge through the enemy that they could use as an avenue of escape.

Another white panel van roared up the street, pushing aside parked vehicles, crushing its own grille against the rear bumper of an ancient Chevy Nova as it moved. The van interposed itself between Bolan and Davis. A shooter in the passenger seat pushed the barrel of a Glock 18 machine pistol from the window and emptied its 33-round magazine at Bolan.

The Executioner hit the ground. The blast burned the air above him. He fired through the door of the van, his .44 slugs finding their mark. The man with the Glock 18 died where he sat.

The driver had a sawed-off shotgun and was jumping out to meet him, as more men emerged from the sliding door. Bolan shot one of them and then the Desert Eagle was empty. He yanked the Beretta free, and the weapon spit 9 mm death through the van's doorway, chopping down enemy shooters like trees.

The shotgunner leveled his weapon and triggered a slug that punched a quarter-size hole in the fender of the nearby Ford. Bolan put a 9 mm hole through the man's forehead in answer.

"Cooper," Davis said over the earbud link, "I've got real trouble here. I'm out of ammunition."

"Stay where you are," Bolan said. "I'll fight my way to you."

"Uh-oh," Davis said.

Bolan could hear the roar of a vehicle. Behind the van nearest him, a third cargo van was closing on Davis's location. Through the earbud link, Bolan could hear the background noise of a van door sliding open. He heard men yelling, then Davis's grunts of protest.

"Get off me!" Davis shouted. The detective was smart enough not to speak directly to Bolan, not to give away that he had a means of communicating with his ally. Bolan came around the van and began shooting at the third vehicle, going for the tires, but the van was already moving and the cars between Bolan and the van stopped the soldier from getting a clear shot at the wheels.

Davis was gone. They had him.

"Dammit," Bolan said. He shot a man in the face.

There were more gunners operating in his vicinity, but they were cagier. Apparently Chamblis had left them behind to perform a holding action. He doubted these men understood they had essentially been sacrificed to cover Chamblis's escape.

His phone began to vibrate. He stabbed the hands-free button, sending the call to his earbud and cutting the signal from Davis's transmitter. There was nothing he could do for Davis until he eliminated the shooters trying to kill him here.

He began weaving among the abandoned vehicles, his Beretta punching 9 mm hollowpoint rounds through man after man.

"Go," Bolan said aloud.

"We've just gotten word through channels," Price said in his ear. "Hal's tried to— Striker, was that a shot?"

The earbud's automatic sound-leveling and heuristics algorithms adjusted the earpiece volume and its microphone gain based on external noise. What Price would be hearing would be the occasional flat, static-laden dead zone that was the earbud cutting out to protect both her and Bolan from the sound of a gunshot nearby.

"Yes," Bolan said. "Barb, I've just lost Detective Davis. He's been abducted by the enemy, a kill team led by Reginald Chamblis."

"So Chamblis is definitely behind it."

"Between your files and my intel," Bolan said, pausing to shoot a man in the throat, "we have enough to put together a video package. I'll dictate as I drive. Hang on, I have to find a car to drive."

Price said nothing. Bolan picked an abandoned Toyota sedan near the outside of the cluster of abandoned cars and trucks. He would dictate the registration to the Farm so they could see to it the driver was compensated. But at the moment, there were more pressing concerns. A gunman tried to sneak up on him as he climbed into the vehicle, using the other cars for concealment, but Bolan saw him in the mirror. He pointed the Beretta behind his own body and fired without turning his head. The man went down. That, the Executioner believed, was the last of them. The car was already running; he shifted and hit the gas, pulling out onto the sidewalk to clear the impromptu traffic jam.

"All right," Bolan said. "Have Aaron and his people transcribe what I'm about to tell you. Cross-reference that with the data we have. Davis has bulletins out on Chamblis and Patrick Farnham. I have reason to believe Farnham went rogue, killing civilians at random rather than biding his time and striking at the fringes. Apparently Chamblis is the leader of a death cult of knife murderers, who have been offing street people and other fringe victims for years. They've been doing so with help from within the Detroit police, including a Detective Slate, now deceased, and a Detective Bill Griffith, now in custody. The rest of what you need should be obvious in the files you've got based on Chamblis's holdings and the address we got from Slovic. Slovic was a member of the cult, apparently. They tried to hide his death in order to prevent us uncovering Chamblis's dueling studio."

"All right, Striker. I think that's everything we need."

"Except whether there's a heroic, dead cop involved." Bolan took his phone from his pocket and selected an application. "I'm going to hang up on you, Barb. I've got to concentrate on following Davis."

"Why do you think they took him?"

"If I were Chamblis," Bolan said, "I'd want to know just how much the other side knows."

"If he's watching the news tonight," Price said, "that won't be a secret. His involvement will be blown wide."

"If he's smart, he'll get out of town before that happens, just on the possibility that it's coming down," Bolan said. "But this revenge play isn't smart, so we don't know that. He'll go somewhere to build a fire under Davis. I've got until the news breaks to get the kid back. They'll kill him either way. Depending on how badly they cut him up to question him, he may not survive even if he lives through it. If you follow me."

"You think they will?"

"Chamblis is cracked," Bolan said. "He'd have to be. We've already seen what happens when one of these knifers goes off the rails."

"Hurry, Striker."

"On it. Out."

Bolan kept one eye on the traffic and the other on his phone. The application booted and loaded for him a map of the area taken from satellite data. Superimposed on this map was a blinking amber dot.

That dot was Adam Davis.

Bolan put his foot down on the accelerator. "Hold on, kid," he said quietly. "The cavalry's coming."

17

Bolan listened as Chamblis prepared to torture Davis.

The Executioner was lying flat on a rooftop overlooking the warehouse in which the detective was held captive. The sun was setting. On televisions throughout the region, news would be breaking of the serial murders. Terror would quickly descend on the city. The only remedy for that terror would be the immediate release by the Farm to local media outlets of a resolution to the crisis.

Bolan was going to force that resolution.

The area looked more or less deserted, as did so many of Detroit's more industrial areas. Chamblis probably owned property here, since he had made a beeline for the spot as soon as Davis was in his clutches. He obviously thought himself safe enough, here, far from any of his obvious holdings and nowhere near the scene of any of the knife killings that Bolan knew about. There were portable lights burning in the warehouse below, illuminating the tableau before Bolan as Chamblis strutted about in front of the seated detective. Davis's wrists and ankles were strapped to the wooden chair in which he sat.

Every detail came to Bolan crisply and clearly through the advanced, variable intensity optics of the John "Cowboy"

Kissinger–tuned M-16/M-203 assault rifle, grenade launcher combo he held snug to his shoulder. Every sound in the warehouse was transmitted through Davis's earbud transceiver, which was small enough and unusual enough that the goons holding the man had not thought to check for it.

"I want guards at every entrance," Chamblis was saying. "Make this place a bunker. No one in or out."

"Yes, Maestro." The man who called Chamblis "Maestro" was apparently some kind of second in command. His name was Andreas. At least, that was what Chamblis called him when he addressed the man.

Chamblis's voice was suddenly louder in Bolan's ear, as the man leaned over the bound Detective Davis, gesturing with a long, wicked-looking knife that he held with easy familiarity. Every so often, Chamblis would take a few steps away and execute some kind of kata or form with the knife, moving it through the air, cutting invisible enemies. Whether this was a tic borne of agitation or evidence that Chamblis was losing it, Bolan could not speculate.

The soldier had closed his phone. The tracking application loaded on to it, combined with its GPS capability, had led the soldier here without difficulty. The tracking device had only limited range, but Bolan had been quick to stay within that range, allowing him to follow Davis across the city. The microdot transmitter was hidden in the *i* of the words *Justice Department* on the business card Bolan had given Davis. The miniaturized transceiver was, like the earbuds, a product of the genius of Hermann "Gadgets" Schwarz.

Bolan had known from the beginning of the mission that he faced corruption and possible betrayal from within the Detroit police. At varying times he had held his own suspicions about Davis, but the man had acquitted himself well throughout this run. It had still seemed prudent, at their first meeting, to slip the man the tracking card. There were many reasons this might prove valuable, the current need to follow and save Davis from the enemy being one of them.

Adam Davis had a guardian angel, and that angel held a rifle chambered for 5.56 mm rounds.

What was more, Davis knew it. Bolan had started talking to Davis not long after the pursuit began, explaining that he had the means to follow and was doing so. Once in position on the roof, he had explained to Davis just where he was and what he was doing. The detective had maintained his cool throughout the ordeal, even when the man named Andreas had roughed him up a little.

"I want to know," Chamblis told Davis, gesturing with his knife, "who you've told, and what you've told them."

"There's a public bulletin out on you and your boy Farnham," Davis told him. "You won't get far if you show your face. I would imagine once they catch you they'll charge you with murder, accessory to murder, conspiracy to commit murder… You know, the usual. The same for Farnham."

"Farnham is a dead issue," Chamblis said smugly.

"You whack him?" Davis asked. Bolan had to appreciate the detective's courage. He was tied to a chair, possibly facing disfigurement at the hands of a knife-wielding madman, with his only assistance a long rifle shot away. Yet he was pumping Chamblis for information knowing that the man he knew as Agent Cooper could hear.

"Normally I would take offense," Chamblis said. "That is such an…inelegant way to put it. But it is, in this case, accurate. Farnham was rabid. I put him out of his misery."

"Farnham," Davis said, "had a brain tumor. He was crazy, all right. Makes you wonder how you two ever had anything in common."

That gave Chamblis pause. "I didn't know," he said. "It would…explain much."

"Oh yeah?" Davis shot back. "It doesn't explain how you

and your personal Manson Family go running around knifing people!"

"Are you really so blind?" Chamblis said. "What do you think? That all men and women are created equal?" He laughed at that. "There is no more simple, perfect, or elegant killing instrument than the blade. In using it, the enlightened warrior gains purity. He gains strength. He gains wisdom."

"Stabbing bums and hookers doesn't make you enlightened," Davis said. "It sure as hell doesn't make you a 'warrior.'"

"Very well, then," Chamblis said angrily. "I will be content simply to be superior materially, you insect. This warehouse and dozens others like it? I own it. Do you have any idea what my net worth is? Do you?"

"Do you think your 'net worth' will be worth much once you're a hunted fugitive?" Davis countered.

"Then I need to know the true extent of the damage," Chamblis said. "Your investigation has obviously been far-reaching, Detective Davis. If you don't want to die screaming for the pain to stop, if you don't want me to flay the skin from your bones, you will tell me exactly what I need to know."

"You're screwed," Davis said simply.

Garter took a step closer and belted Davis across the face. "You will use respect when you address the Maestro!" he shouted. "Or I will cut your throat myself!"

Davis straightened himself. The kid had guts. Bolan could see it in the man's face through the scope.

"In a few seconds," Bolan said quietly, "I'm going to turn off the lights."

"I understand," Davis said. Garter nodded, believing Davis had been cowed.

"Oh, and Andreas?" Davis said.

"What?"

"Your Maestro can go fuck himself."

Bolan pulled the trigger. The 5.56 mm NATO round

punched a neat hole in Garter's forehead. He staggered, dead on his feet, before toppling.

Chamblis opened his mouth, but made no sounds. He turned bright red.

"Go," Bolan said.

Davis threw himself to the floor, taking the chair with him. Bolan began shooting out the lights. He did it in rapid succession, acquiring targets as quickly as any human being could, his veteran sniper skills pushed to the limit as he plunged the warehouse into calculated, successive darkness. Then, with Davis's position on the floor burned into his memory, he swapped 30-round magazines and flicked the selector switch on the customized rifle.

Bolan pulled back the M-16's trigger and held it there, blazing away in a broad arc and he held the weapon level on its attached bipod and walked the barrel across his field of fire. He heard, through Davis's earpiece, the sound of men screaming and dying. Somewhere in the midst of that he heard the sound of Chamblis roaring his outrage.

Bolan had used, taken from his war bag, a grappling hook and coil of rope to climb to his perch on the adjacent building. Through the many wide and broken windows of the darkened warehouse he could see the muzzle-flashes of small-arms fire. The gunmen were firing wildly, disoriented. They had no way of knowing from where the threat had come. Even if they managed to put together what had just taken place, Bolan would not be there for them to find or hunt.

He reached his grappling hook, tested its hold on the lip of the building and half slid, half rappelled down the side of the building with his rifle slung over his shoulder. Once at ground level he unslung the M-16 and set the variable optics for close-range red dot. Kissinger had done his lethal work well. The rifle felt like a part of Bolan as the soldier brought it up before him, combat ready.

He crossed the street in the deepening shadows, making

for the closest entrance. There would be men guarding that entry, probably with weapons poised to gun down any man who stepped through the double doors.

Bolan launched a 40 mm high explosive grenade at the entrance.

The distance from Davis's position was within safety guidelines. The explosion splintered the doors with enough force to kill anyone who might be hiding behind it or nearby. Bolan took a pair of compact night-vision goggles from his war bag. He put them to his eyes, switched them on and stepped into the hell he was about to create.

Armed men, some in uniform and some not, ran everywhere. In the midst of all of this, in green and black hues, Bolan could see Chamblis. The man was on his knees in the dark, searching for Davis. He was stabbing the floor with his knife every pace or so. Davis was not in the direct path of the man's blind fumbling, but he soon would be. In his earpiece, Bolan could hear Davis's heavy breathing.

Bolan aimed the rifle, a process made slightly more awkward by the goggles he wore. He settled the weapon's sights on Chamblis's forehead....

The blow that chopped his feet out from under him was completely unexpected. Bolan went down in a tangle of limbs. One of the gunmen had blundered into him in the darkness and somehow identified him as foe rather than friend. The soldier was suddenly on the ground, his adversary on top of him, raining down punches from above. Both men had lost their guns in the confusion.

Bolan arched his back slightly, repositioning himself onto his side beneath his foe. It was adjustment enough that he could draw the Desert Eagle from its holster. With the weapon pressed against his own body, angled up and into his attacker, he fired several rounds from retention. The muzzle-blasts scorched his abdomen but had the desired effect. His enemy was perforated again and again until he went slack and collapsed next to Bolan, who surged to his feet.

He had the advantage of sight in a kingdom of otherwise blind men. Bolan snatched up the M-16 once more and swept the room. Chamblis was not visible. Davis was still on the floor. He seemed to be throwing a thumbs-up sign into the darkness.

"Davis?" Bolan said.

"I'm fine!" the detective said. "He went that way!" Davis pointed. "I heard his steps!"

Bolan took note of the detective's orientation. The fight wasn't over. Under these conditions, however, it was not a fight so much as it was a slaughter. The soldier was no butcher. He was, instead, a hunter, removing predators wherever he found them. He locked on targets and then eliminated them.

This was a target-rich environment.

Bolan stalked the enemy gunners through the darkness like a wraith. There was plenty of cover in the warehouse: crates, abandoned machinery, contours within the irregular flooring that were deep enough, in some spots, to shield a crouching man or drop him to injury and death. As the gunmen scattered, ineffectual without their leader, Bolan hunted them. Each time his M-16 barked, it sent tremors of fear through the thugs who remained.

A man stood in Bolan's path, his shotgun swinging wildly. Bolan took him down.

A second gunner crouch-walked across the Executioner's field of fire, triggering random bursts from a Heckler & Koch submachine gun. He succeeded in killing two of his fellow hired guns before Bolan finally put a 5.56 mm round through his brain.

A third would-be killer teetered at the edge of one of the pits in the floor. Bolan walked past him and simply pushed him in. Something cracked when the man hit bottom.

The Executioner ran among his foes and took them out one and two at a time, emptying one, then a second magazine. He loaded a third and swept the warehouse a final time, making sure he had missed no one.

The soldier finally worked his way past Davis. He crouched, pulling the Sting combat dagger from his belt, and cut the straps holding Davis to his chair. The detective began massaging his wrists and ankles.

"That was close," he said. "He was going to cut my throat."

"I won't stop for coffee next time," Bolan said without expression.

"Yeah," Davis said. "Yeah, that's good."

"I've got to go after him. Can you run?"

"No—" Davis shook his head "—my legs feel dead. I'd only hold you up. Go, Cooper. While you can still catch him."

Bolan nodded. "Davis."

"Yeah?"

"You're a good cop."

The Executioner hurried on.

18

The warehouse opened up into a crumbling freight complex, a relic of a Detroit that once built and manufactured great things. Like so many manufacturing centers, Detroit's greatest years had passed it by, and these blocks of decaying buildings, once devoted to storing items of value before they were shipped from the city, stood in mute testimony to the changing of economic paradigms.

Night had fallen completely. The sky was cloud covered, reflecting the light of the city to form an ephemeral amber backdrop. Bolan crouched. He had removed the night-vision goggles. Here, outside the close confines of the warehouse, his human senses were best, for he had logged countless hours as a jungle fighter under similar conditions. Whether in the glass-and-steel canyons of urban battlegrounds, or surrounded by the humidity of tropical climates and jungle foliage, there was no more effective soldier than Bolan.

There were only two possibilities: a man so bent on revenge that he had deferred his escape despite the knowledge that he was publicly wanted had turned and fled after his initial defeat here, or this was a trap. It seemed likely that Chamblis would be lying in wait for him out there, somewhere in the darkness. The only question was whether he was

alone. Men like Chamblis, so falsely brave when they held all
the cards, were often cowards when the odds were more even.

The gunman screwed up. The shot that echoed across the
abandoned warehouse complex kicked up cracked paving at
Bolan's feet but never came close to injuring him. The soldier
took cover behind a rusted-out forklift whose tires were flat.
The heavy metal machine absorbed a sudden hail of bullets
as automatic gunfire ripped the night.

Bolan crouched, calmly, waiting and listening. He detected
two, no, three sources of gunfire. The rattle of automatic
weaponry sang a dissonant song; no two instruments were
ever quite completely in tune with each other.

He flipped the M-16's selector switch to single shot and
loaded a fresh 40 mm grenade. In the darkness, he would be
snap-shooting with the launcher, making each shot his best
guess—but close was often close enough when it came to
high explosives. Bolan waited for the forklift to rock under
another wave of gunfire. He timed the next lull, popped up,
leveled the weapon and triggered the grenade.

The red-orange blossom of flame cast flickering shadows
and left flashes in his vision. It also illuminated a second of
his attackers, this one a man in a crimson uniform. Bolan
fired a single shot that drilled his target through the left eye,
spraying brain through an exit wound notably larger than the
diameter of the 5.56 mm round that had made it. The soft-
nosed rounds were perfect antipersonnel ammunition, lov-
ingly loaded by Kissinger himself.

At least, Bolan thought, the question of whether Chamblis
had brought backup was answered. There had been a small
army in the warehouse. The soldier had no doubt that Chamblis would bring as many gunners with him as he had been
able to draw and retain. The men left behind in the warehouse
had been merely a diversion, a delaying tactic. Chamblis had
left them on the floor of a killing ground to cover his with-
drawal to a more advantageous position.

The open ground in front of Bolan widened, then nar-rowed, then widened in a recurring pattern. The pattern was not deliberate; it was the by-product of the way ancient cargo containers and abandoned machinery had been pushed into groups by whoever had cleared more salable merchandise from this property. The gaps between what had been left behind were roughly the size of a tractor-trailer, which made perfect sense from a freight-moving standpoint.

It created a problem. Bolan would have to cross a series of open killing fields. There was no shortage of vantages from which his enemies could fire on him. He was one man, alone, facing many. They had a higher position and knew precisely where he was.

Bolan had faced worse odds.

Rifle held against his chest, he ran across the first gap. The first one was always something of a "give me," for the enemy would not be expecting a simple charge across open ground. Bullets chewed the pavement after him, and Bolan made the gunmen's job more difficult by taking an erratic path across the terrain while keeping his speed high. He cleared the gap and took shelter behind a metal cargo con-tainer, which rang like a gong as bullets struck it.

There was no point delaying. He did the same for the next gap. The shots came closer to him this time, but he was fi-nally able to do something about it. He could see the muzzle-flashes in the darkness, Bolan's charge making him a target tempting enough that the gunmen broke cover to take him down.

The M-16 came up against Bolan's shoulder. He adopted a half run, half glide, keeping his rifle on target and his lower body stable while maintaining his forward movement. The enemy gunmen almost had his range, but when Bolan re-turned fire—in the form of methodical single shots, each one aimed with care—he began to drive them back. Suddenly the enemy had more than just killing him on their minds—they had to save themselves.

He took one gunman in the head. He shot another in the chest and drilled a third in the neck. It was, for the Executioner, as natural as breathing. He kept running.

A disturbing creak under his feet told him that he was no longer on solid ground. He flashed the weapon light of the M-16 on the ground, briefly, moving as he did so. He drew no fire, for he was behind cover, but the light told him what he needed to know. He was walking on planks of heavy, aged wood.

The warehouse complex either was built into a natural declination, or there was a pit or subbasement built under it. Platforms of wood had, long ago, been built atop it. Bolan kept going, but his footsteps were currently making too much noise as he ran. The creaking and the hollow thump of his boots on the planks was enough to draw that much more automatic weapon fire. He poured on the speed.

At the next juncture he pressed himself against a stack of empty metal drums. Bullets sparked against them; Chamblis's men were really not sparing their ammunition. Bolan judged the angle of the shots and knew he was in trouble. They were coming from high up. A quick glance confirmed that, yes, there was an old crane gantry to the southwest. He could see muzzle-flashes from behind a metal screen, probably once intended to protect the crane operator, it presently fouled any shot he might take at the sniper high above him.

That crow's-nest position would have to be eliminated or Bolan would not get much farther. He took a 90-degree detour toward the tower, his sudden change of course startling a few of the gunmen who had been preparing to meet his next crossing. Bolan targeted their muzzle-flashes, squeezing short, tight blasts from the M-16, clustering his shots to make up for the snap-shooting he was forced to do on the run.

He was rewarded with more cries of panic and pain. His rounds were finding their mark. With each wave he was reducing the odds against him, chipping away at Chamblis's forces. The only problem was that a smart man would use this, too, as a delaying tactic. While Bolan painstakingly took out each tier of Chamblis's henchmen, it was possible that the man himself was making a fast getaway.

Once again, Bolan vowed to find Chamblis wherever he might hide, should he escape this night.

As he made for the rusted crane, the sniper took aim at him. He dodged, rolled and came up running again. A bullet creased his thigh, but he kept moving, barely feeling the familiar burn of the bullet.

More bullets began to ricochet from the crane gantry as the frustrated sniper tried to fire straight down, through the steel struts supporting him in his perch. To climb into that would be suicide; Bolan needed a diversion. He loaded a 40 mm grenade, this one an incendiary, and triggered the launcher.

The grenade smashed into the struts immediately below the top of the crane gantry. The gantry shook, but the weathered steel held. Flames rose high, blinding and startling the sniper. As the Executioner jumped onto the crane and began to climb the rickety ladder leading upward, he held the M-16 in one hand, the muzzle pointing skyward.

He could have used an HE grenade to destroy the crane from farther away, but he did not want to destroy it. He wanted to claim the crow's-nest position for himself.

The sniper was recovering when Bolan gained the top of the crane gantry. He rolled over the lip of the top of the platform, yanked the Sting knife from his waistband and plunged it in the sniper's throat. He ripped the blade over and down. A shower of blood rained through the grate of the platform. The soldier shoved the dead sniper's body over the edge of the landing with a well-placed kick. There was a Ruger Mini-30 with a scope on the platform. The soldier left it where it lay.

Bolan's night-vision goggles were compatible with the variable optics of his rifle. Kissinger would not have put together the armament package for Bolan if they were not. Everything that had made the sniper a difficult target also protected Bolan, and that had been his aim. He snapped open the M-16's attached bipod, stretched himself out and put the rifle to his shoulder. On the ground, in the open, he had wanted to hear, to smell, to see the enemy with his own eyes. But from high above, technology was his advantage.

He began with movement. No man in a firefight, or under the threat of one, could bring himself to be completely, utterly still. Few men had the talent, and those who did made superb snipers…like Bolan. The Executioner waited for the telltale wavers in the greens and blacks of his field of vision, knowing the slight restlessness all men felt in combat would eventually betray his foes.

He did not have to wait long. Bolan found his first target, drew in a breath, let out half of that breath and squeezed the trigger. It was muscle memory for him, a movement as practiced as walking and as effortless as sleeping. The bullet screamed down from above with the sharp crack so familiar to any who had fired the AR-15/M-16 family of firearms. When it found its mark, it bored a neat hole above the bridge of one of the previously hidden gunmen's nose.

The enemy reacted with panic fire. They were shooting in his general direction, with some vague notion that the threat was currently above them, that their advantage, their ace in the sky, had been co-opted.

None of the bullets were near him. Bolan was in no danger. He began to walk the rifle slowly from his left to his right. Each time he found a target, he fired once. One shot, one kill was the old motto; he did it justice.

"Cooper." Davis's voice was in his earbud. "Do you need assistance?"

"Stay where you are," Bolan said. "I've got night vision out here. You'd be walking into this blind, and Chamblis has gunners waiting."

"What is your status?"

"Thinning the herd," Bolan said. He pulled the trigger and another man died. "Evening the odds."

"I'm calling this in," Davis stated.

"Do it," Bolan said. "But warn them that they'll be walking into a war zone. Multiple hostiles, automatic weapons. If they roll, roll the local equivalent of SWAT."

"Understood."

The Executioner kept at his deadly work. The pace of his hunting slowed as he began to do serious damage to the enemy. He did not see Chamblis, but in truth at this distance and under these light levels, even with the scope of his rifle, he would be hard pressed to identify the man or differentiate him from his hired help.

He picked off two more shooters. Finally, though, he was out of obvious targets. It was time to leave his perch. Before he did so, he took the magazine from the Ruger and tossed it over the side. He also grabbed the scope and wrenched it hard to one side, fouling its zero. He did not, as a general rule, leave functioning weapons behind him. He would have liked to do a more thorough job on the Ruger but he did not dare take the time. This would be enough.

He climbed back down the ladder. His boots hit the rotting timbers beneath him heavily; he heard them creak and heave and wondered precisely how old the planks were. Pushing his night-vision goggles up off his face, he crouched low, breathing in the cool night air and making as small a target of himself as possible. He used the night sky, so much lighter than most people thought it to be, to silhouette any enemy who might be moving. It was an old combat technique sometimes thought to have originated with the ninja, the feudal Japanese assassins. Bolan didn't worry himself over ancient history. It was simply a function of how the world worked, from physics to optics.

Once more in a gliding crouch with his weapon shouldered, he stalked forward. Every sense he had was open to the night; every sound, every gust of wind, he sensed and evaluated. Moving silently, he kept on, knowing that at the end of the complex, where the buildings narrowed once more and the space between them diminished to almost nothing, he would either find Chamblis or he would come up empty.

When he had moved thirty paces and drawn no fire, he knew it was time to force the issue, to make it happen on his terms rather than on those of the enemy. He stopped.

"Reginald Chamblis!" he yelled. His voice echoed across the old cargo containers. "Reginald Chamblis!"

A voice finally answered him. "They're all dead."

"Come out, Chamblis! You'll never leave the city. Surrender and live!"

"Surrender and live," Chamblis's voice echoed back. Bolan could not fix it; he thought Chamblis was somewhere ahead and on the left, but he could not be sure. He held the M-16 before his body at a low ready. "What a perfectly predictable philosophy you have."

"You're a murderer, Chamblis," Bolan said. "Nothing more. You think a knife in your hand makes you a predator? You think this is a game, with rules you can dictate? It isn't. You don't understand this world, Chamblis." He was deliberately taunting the man, using a personal version of the strategy and tactics that had served him on this mission.

Elsewhere in the city, it was Halloween. Children would be going from door to door collecting candy, with nothing more serious on their minds than how big their hauls might be. Here, in this place, life and death would be settled in fractions of a second. Bolan would do that settling. Once more, he was judge, he was jury…and he was executioner.

Chamblis stepped out of hiding.

He was holding something in his hand behind his body. Bolan brought the barrel of the rifle up and on target. It was an easy shot, a shot he could have made even while point-shooting. At this distance, simply swinging the barrel in Chamblis's general direction, by reflex, would put the contents of Bolan's magazine into the man's chest. But Chamblis seemed strangely unafraid.

He had a knife in his hand.

"I only wanted to learn," Chamblis said. "The search for knowledge. It's a noble thing, isn't it, Cooper? Cooper isn't even your real name, is it?"

"Does it matter?" Bolan asked.

"No," Chamblis said. "Only, I've been in bed with the Mafia for a long time, Cooper. It was a means to an end. Did you know the mafiosi, those brave underworld crime figures? Do you know they have a bogeyman?"

"I wasn't aware," Bolan said. "Put your hands where I can see them."

"They do," Chamblis said. "They whisper it. They tell tall tales around their campfires, or whatever it is men like that sit around. Gas-powered fireplaces, perhaps. Maybe even outdoor grills. How quaint."

"Get on the deck," Bolan ordered.

Still Chamblis ignored him. "They tell stories about a man who killed hundreds, no, thousands of their kind," Chamblis said. "They're terrified of him. They seem to think he can take on scores of men, hundreds of men, single-handed, emerging victorious walking over a pile of bodies each time. Imagine that! Does that make any sense to you? Does it sound plausible?" Chamblis's voice became a low whisper. "Do you know anything about that, Cooper?"

"Can't say I do," Bolan said.

"Pity," Chamblis said. "I was curious." He whipped his arm from behind his body and threw something at Bolan.

The grenade, its spoon already popped free, landed at Bolan's feet.

The Executioner snapped off a shot that found its mark, judging from the pained grunt Chamblis made. Bolan jumped up and away, trying to push himself backward using the rifle as leverage. He held the weapon before him as the bomb exploded.

The concussion hit him, driving the wind from his lungs, knocking him onto his back. He tried to take the brunt of it in a controlled fall, slapping his arm to absorb some of the blow. The M-16 exploded in a shower of plastic shards. While the receiver was intact, the rest of the weapon was dealt heavy damage by proximity to the grenade. Bolan would not be using that gun again, not this time out.

Something cracked. He realized what was happening only as it became too late.

Beneath him, the plank floor gave way.

19

Bolan fell. The tiers of planking onto which the terminus of the cargo complex was built was crumbling, breaking away, giving in to years of neglect and natural rot and, perhaps, even lowest-bidder union workmanship. The damage done by Chamblis's grenade had dealt the structure a fatal blow. It could not support the weight of the men and equipment atop it, not once the explosion had ripped out its guts.

Bolan could not stop his tumble. He was rolling, he was falling, he was turning and rolling again. He felt something heavy and sharp slam into his torso, something that sent shock waves of pain through his body as alarm bells were triggered in his nervous system.

He smashed his head against a rough section of timber, slapped an arm hard against another plank, and then hit with a bone-jarring thud on his back at the bottom of what seemed a skyscraper of wooden debris. He tasted blood and felt a stiffness in his neck. Bright spots danced in front of his vision.

He remembered seeing the M-16 destroyed by the grenade blast. He reached for his Beretta, but it was not there. His shoulders were very sore, and suddenly he remembered the leather harness catching on something on the way down. The harness had been ripped from his back. His pistol was gone.

The double-edged Sting knife was still in his waistband, as was his Desert Eagle in its Kydex sheath. His war bag was gone, however, and with it most of his ammunition. The bag had been ripped free by the fall, which had probably torn the heavy canvas shoulder strap loose.

Before he tried to move, he eased the Desert Eagle from its Kydex sheath. His left hand was not of much help when he checked the magazine, for his thumb appeared to be broken. It sent shrieking signals of pain at him whenever he tried to bend it.

The Desert Eagle was chambered and held a total of eight rounds. He put it back in its holster, for as much as he wanted to have it at the ready, he needed to assess his other injuries. His thumb throbbed.

"Cooper!" Davis's voice was very tinny in his ear. The distance at which Davis lay was either too far for the range of the little transceivers, or something about the debris surrounding Bolan was blocking the signal. Davis tried a few more times, but his voice was getting quieter, not louder. Eventually it stopped altogether.

Bolan was on his own.

He tried to move and was racked with pain. Looking down, he realized what the problem was. A shard of wood, the length of his forearm and two inches wide, projected from his abdomen.

His mind quickly scrolled through his battlefield first-aid options and discarded most of them. His first-aid kit was with his war bag, now gone. He had a smaller pocket kit with him, but it would be of little use for a wound this severe. He decided that despite the general complications associated with removing an object on which one was impaled, he would not be able to function with this length of timber jutting from his body. With his good right hand, he wrenched the piece of wood free.

The pain was so intense that he saw a rainbow of colors, which threatened to swamp him as he drifted dangerously close to unconsciousness. He could not afford that. If Chamblis were still here, somewhere, alive—

"Hello, Cooper." Chamblis appeared above him. "That's a nasty looking wound you've got there."

Bolan tried to roll quickly out of the way, but bones ground against bone within his rib cage. He steeled himself against the pain, but it was too late. The reaction had slowed him. Chamblis was on top of him, tearing the Desert Eagle from his holster. Bolan attempted to retain the pistol, but he was fighting with one arm. Chamblis drew his knife and slashed Bolan across the right hand, creating just enough give to yank the Desert Eagle free.

"That doesn't look good, Cooper," Chamblis gloated. "You've got some cracked ribs, I'm willing to bet. Never an easy injury to tolerate."

Bolan scissored his legs up and over, ignoring the pain. He slammed his right fist into Chamblis's face, leaving a smear of his own blood. Chamblis came back and grabbed his left hand, wrenching the thumb hard.

Blinding white light flooded Bolan's eyes, a lightning bolt of pain. There was an audible pop. As quickly as the pain came, it dissipated. Before Bolan could act Chamblis kicked him in the face, knocking him backward. Bolan rolled onto his stomach, desperately trying to push to his feet once more. Every combat instinct he had screamed at him to get up, to get off the ground, to get mobile so he could once again engage the enemy. His mind, so skilled in the methods of warfare, knew precisely what he had to do. His body, however, had limitations, as did any mortal man's. Bolan was, thanks to the explosion and fall, very near his threshold for physical abuse.

"Your thumb was dislocated, Cooper," Chamblis said. "I've just fixed it for you. Don't worry, I'll send you a bill."

Bolan was in real trouble. Chamblis had gone over the edge into complete hysteria. He also was not unscathed from the explosion that had dropped both men to this depth. He had a nasty wound across his forehead and cheek that would, if he lived, leave him disfigured for life. He was also favoring one foot, although not so much that it affected his mobility. It was not a weakness Bolan would be able to exploit in his current condition.

In his position on all fours, Bolan knew his damaged ribs made too tempting a target for someone like Chamblis to resist. As his opponent came in, Bolan used his arms to grab the incoming kick, blunting some of its force. The savage blow still rocked him, however, taking his wind and forcing him to grab Chamblis's leg to prevent a follow-up.

"This," Chamblis said, "is not how we're going to do this." He kicked Bolan in the face again, catching him under the chin. It was a glancing blow, but it hurt. The soldier flipped over onto his back and stared up at the nighttime sky, far above. Then Chamblis was invading his field of vision again.

"We are going to duel, Agent Cooper. I am going to take your life in honorable combat." Chamblis tucked the Desert Eagle into his belt behind his back. "Damn you, I will teach you what it is I and my fellowship have worked so hard to achieve. You will understand, before you die. Devil take you, you will understand!"

"You're living in a fantasy world, Chamblis," Bolan said. "You think because you and your fellow madmen got together and stabbed innocent men and women, you're a fellowship? Some twisted idea of a church or a fraternity? You're predators."

"Yes!" Chamblis said. "You do understand. We are predators. We take prey. We take the weak. We control. We do. We are."

"You're nuts," Bolan said. He was still lying on his back; Chamblis was making no attempt to move in. The crazed cult leader held his bowie knife tightly in his right hand. Blood dripped slowly from the terrible gash in his face.

"People like you are so quick to defame and denigrate what they cannot understand," Chamblis said. "Look at you, Cooper. You're a thug. Why, you're a mass murderer! How many people have you killed today, Cooper?"

"Funny," Bolan said, "but I don't remember killing anybody who wasn't trying to murder me first."

"Isn't that always the refuge of the scoundrel?" Chamblis said. "'They made me do it. It was some other fellow's idea. He started it.'"

"Self-defense," Bolan said, "is all *about* who started it."

"Philosophy, now, Agent Cooper? I didn't know you had it in you."

"You're not nearly as intelligent as you think you are," Bolan said. "Predators never are. You take what you want from those weaker. You attack only those against whom you know you can win. You tell yourself you're risking something, or standing for something, or accomplishing something. You're not doing any of those things. In his heart, every societal predator is just a scared little bully, trying to take something he hasn't earned because he wants it."

"You won't speak to me that way," Chamblis said. "I am an honorable, worthy foe! You will treat me with respect!"

"Respect?" Bolan asked. "Does a garbage man respect the squirrels rooting around in the trash cans? Does a doctor respect a rash? I don't respect you, Chamblis. You may think you're some kind of new-age warrior, some kind of figure of action and drama. You're not. You're a bully. A scared little boy with a weapon in his hand, an attitude on his face and a chip on his shoulder. You were nothing when you started and you'll end as nothing. You're going to pay for what you've done."

"Who's going to make me?" Chamblis said. "You?"

"It's payday," Bolan said.

"I know what you're trying to do," Chamblis said. "You forget I am no amateur. You are trying to goad me. You're a dangerous man, Agent Cooper. Perhaps the most evil man I've ever met. You will not take me so easily as you took all the others."

"Come and get it, then," Bolan said. "But you'd better hurry. I'm getting damned tired of hearing you talk. I have to admit I'd like to shut you up myself."

Chamblis snapped. He came in, trying for a kick, a grab, or even a slash with his knife. Bolan used his training. He pivoted on his back, using one of his legs as a drive leg, the other extended to ward off Chamblis. Whenever Chamblis came in, Bolan shot a vicious pistoning sidekick into the man's shin. He had to suck up his own pair.

Chamblis tried to stomp him, but the outcome was the same. Bolan almost broke the shin clean, that time. On a man with less training and conditioning, more than a few of the blows would have snapped bone. Chamblis, however, was both too tough and too smart to be taken down like that.

"You have training," Chamblis said. "You are really a very accomplished fighter. I saw it in you the moment I first saw you move. You could be one of us, Cooper! You could learn the discipline of the blade. It's not too late. I could teach you."

Bolan was sick and tired of hearing Chamblis talk. He permitted an opening, and when Chamblis shot in, hoping perhaps to get into Bolan's guard and then pass it to mount and stab or punch him, Bolan grabbed the tactical flashlight from his pocket.

The combat light was a cylinder of knurled aluminum the length of Bolan's palm. The Executioner held it in his fist and then, when Chamblis got within range, Bolan rammed the end of the light into the side of Chamblis's skull with every bit of force he could.

Chamblis went limp. He collapsed next to Bolan, out cold.

"At least," he said out loud, gritting his teeth against the pain, "he stopped talking."

Bolan tried to move, but for several moments the pain of his various wounds held him immobile. Finally, he was able to push himself back to his feet, despite the agony emanating from his ribs and the bloody wound in his flank. The wound did not seem to be bleeding too quickly, all things considered; nothing too vital had been punctured.

He pulled his secure satellite phone out of his pocket. It was smashed. The device was rugged, but it, too, had its limitations, and it had never been intended to withstand something like the abuse it had been dealt. Bolan put the device back in his pocket. He could replace the phone itself with a commercial unit by swapping the coded sim card. That would not, however, do him any good at this moment. He was a long way from a box store or gift shop.

He looked up at the lip of the pit into which he and Chamblis had fallen. It was not going to be easy getting back up there.

Then there was Chamblis.

Bolan could see little choice in the matter. He was not going to execute an unconscious man. Chamblis, finally defeated, would have to face the consequences of his crimes.

But they would have to get out of this damned hole first.

Bolan took a step forward and got down to the task at hand. He reclaimed his Desert Eagle from Chamblis's belt, holstered it and grabbed the man's belt with his left arm. Using his right arm, he began pulling himself up through the many hand- and footholds available in the debris.

It was slow going. Like climbing a ladder one-handed, Bolan had to stop with every step, establishing his grip before changing the position of his feet. Several times, debris that seemed solid to his grasp came loose when the weight of two full-size men was balanced against it. Bolan dragged the deadweight of the unconscious Chamblis behind him, not trusting the man over his shoulder. He didn't think his ribs would take that, and he didn't want Chamblis waking up in that position, ready to fight. This way, if Chamblis tried to fight him, he could simply drop the man back into the pit.

"Cooper!" It was Davis's voice in his earbud. The signal was getting stronger as he climbed.

"Cooper...here," Bolan breathed. "Chamblis...in custody. Coming out."

"I know," Davis said. "I'm looking right at you."

Bolan turned his eyes to the lip of the pit and saw a concerned Davis looking down. He kept climbing. He could tell that Davis wanted nothing more than to come down and assist, but that would put them both at risk, with no way to determine how solid the debris leading back to the top was. Bolan's hands were sweating as the stress of his climb and the pain in his chest grew worse.

Finally, he made the top.

"I've got you, I've got you," Davis said. He grabbed Bolan and hauled the man over the edge, careful to drag Chamblis along for the ride. "Wait," Davis said. "He's caught on something. Hang on, I've got to try and...here, Cooper, give me your arm. This won't do. He's hung up down there. I say drop the bastard."

"The thought," Bolan said, "had occurred to me."

Bolan managed to help Davis get a firm grip on Chamblis. They dragged the man over the edge.

Chamblis's eyes snapped open. He was holding Bolan's leather shoulder rig in his hands, having discovered it along the way.

"Look out!" Bolan said. He pushed Davis as far from Chamblis as he could.

The crazed duelist ripped the Beretta from the shoulder leather, drawing down on Bolan. It was the unfamiliar safety mechanism that saved both Bolan and Davis from an untimely death then and there. By the time Chamblis had figured out how to operate the safety, Bolan was pointing the Desert Eagle at him.

Stalemate.

Both men slowly stood. Davis stood as well. His hand started to move for the pistol in his belt, which he had to have recovered from the warehouse. Chamblis shook his head.

"Go for that gun, Detective Davis," Chamblis said, "and I will put a bullet in Agent Cooper. It's only a stalemate if you don't join in. Interfere and we'll have the climax to a nonlinear pop-culture action drama on our hands. Nobody wants that."

"I see you've found a sense of humor," Davis said.

"Quiet!" Chamblis barked. "Two fingers. Take the gun from your belt and put it on the deck. Now!"

Davis looked to Bolan, who nodded. "Go ahead, Davis. I've got this."

"It is I who have you," Chamblis corrected. "Do not forget that, Cooper. I said we were going to duel, and we are."

"You can still live through this," Davis said. "You're committing suicide, Chamblis. Put the gun down."

"This is not suicide," Chamblis said. "This is the final rational act of the most sane man you will ever know."

"Somehow," Bolan said, "I doubt that very much."

"I know how good you are with a gun, Cooper," Chamblis said. "We will lower our weapons simultaneously. Don't think I don't know just how well you are able to shoot without aiming properly. I've watched you do it. Follow along with me, and I will give you the chance to meet me with a blade in my hand. Your friend Davis here can then shoot me or arrest me…once the duel is *over*."

"You're on," Bolan said. He lowered the .44 Magnum handcannon a fraction of an inch.

Chamblis mirrored Bolan's movements. Finally, when the two men held their weapons low enough that a shot from either would not be immediately lethal, Chamblis had another suggestion.

"On the count of three," Chamblis said, "reverse your weapon. Prepare to hand it to me butt-first. I will do the same. We can then draw our knives as we hand our pistols to young Davis, here. What say you, Davis? Does that sound fair?"

"I think it sounds like you've gone completely crackers," Davis said. "But it's your show, Chamblis."

"Yes," Chamblis said. "My show. On three, Cooper. One. Two. Three." Both men reversed their weapons.

"Simple enough," Bolan said. "Now be true to your word, Chamblis. If your honor means anything to you."

"Please," Chamblis said. "Do you think I am so shallow that I need such childish goading to keep my word?"

Chamblis reached for his knife.

Bolan's finger was hooked in the trigger guard of his pistol. In a maneuver known as the Road Agent Spin, he quickly flipped the weapon on the axis of his finger, rolling it up and over into firing position again. Chamblis's eyes widened.

Bolan shot him.

Chamblis's gun hit the planks beneath him. He collapsed to his knees. He was shot in the lung; the maneuver Bolan had used didn't permit much in the way of aiming. Blood bubbled up from the duelist's mouth and leaked down his chin.

"You...you... Why would you..."

"I'm not bound by your rules, Chamblis," Bolan told him. "You're not calling the shots. All those people you murdered were given the same chance I just gave you, which is none at all. You think you can demand consideration? You demand nothing. You get nothing."

"But...honor..." Chamblis whispered.

"What honor is there in a consensual duel?" Bolan said.

"I'm not here to duel you. I'm not here to make you feel good about yourself. I'm here to stop you. To take you out."

Chamblis collapsed, folding backward on rubbery knees that could no longer support him. He smiled as he started to cough. Blood stained his chin and shirt. Then he started to laugh. It was a disconcerting, death-rattle laugh, a sardonic bark. Bolan walked over to stand above the dying man.

"What's so funny?" Davis asked from where he stood.

"At least…" Chamblis said. "At least…I wasn't…*bored*."

The madness faded from Reginald Chamblis's eyes.

He was dead.

Bolan drove with his secure phone's speaker mode activated. The rental car, another Dodge Charger, was pleasantly responsive as he turned the wheel. The engine growled. The sun was setting again. Bolan had spent most of the day in a private room at the local hospital, getting the best care the local medical establishment—as prodded by both Brognola and Barbara Price—could supply.

He was stiff and sore, but it was only the next day, after all. He bore a fairly impressive inventory of stitches, staples, bandages and tape, the latter wrapped around his cracked ribs and around the dressings in his flank. The stitches on his right hand were ugly but would heal without a scar. His other wounds were, at least in his mind, superficial. While he looked at the moment as if he'd been rolled down a hill in a barrel full of gravel, he would heal. He could not say the same for Chamblis, who had been dead on arrival at the same hospital where Bolan was treated.

Brognola was updating him on the remaining details of his recent mission.

"You were right, Striker," he said. "Patrick Farnham's body was found in the same parking garage he used for the last of his murders."

"Knifed?" Bolan asked.

"No," Brognola said. "Shot. A lot. They killed him and then some. An execution with a lot of anger behind it."

"Makes sense," Bolan said. "Farnham broke free of Chamblis's dueling cult and ruined everything for all of them."

"All of them, yeah," Brognola said. "Thanks to Barb and her team, we were on top of Chamblis's assets as soon as the bulletins went out on him. The locals, with help from a detachment of FBI we encouraged along, caught up with a planeload of young men and women waiting to take their private jet to parts unknown."

"Let me guess," Bolan said. "The jet belongs to Reginald Chamblis."

"The same," Brognola said. "They're being held now. We're calling it protective custody, but in reality we just need to ferret out enough data to connect them all directly to Chamblis. Once that's done, it should be relatively easy to interrogate them and get them to roll over on each other."

"Good," Bolan said. "I think we can say the loose ends have been tied up."

"The President of course extends his thanks," Brognola said. "I think he wasn't sure whether to be relieved or disappointed that this wasn't some new terrorist method."

"Disappointed?" Bolan asked. "Why?"

"Because at least if it was, it would mean we knew what to expect, that we'd nailed down what their next tack would be. Can you blame him?"

"No," Bolan said. "Not at all. I understand how he feels."

"As do I. By the way, I'm looking at the e-mail you sent from your hospital bed this morning. I know better than to ask you if you mean this."

"Of course I do," Bolan said.

"Consider it done. Detective Adam Davis will be receiving a commendation for valor, and perhaps even a phone call from the Man himself."

"Good," Bolan said again. "He's earned it."

"Any word on the young detective?"

"He stopped in to see me this morning," Bolan said. "He's a good kid. Reminds me of Johnny."

"Don't they all, the eager ones," Brognola said quietly. Less subdued, he said, "What are you still doing in Detroit, Striker?"

"Those loose ends," Bolan said. "I lied. There's one last one. It won't take long. Then I'll be catching a plane back to the Farm for some R and R."

"Good," Brognola said. "Maybe we can have a chat about the nasty letter from a rental car company this morning."

"Tell them to run me a tab," Bolan said. "Striker out."

Brognola acknowledged Bolan's sign-off and hung up. It was, the soldier thought, the most upbeat mood he had heard expressed by the big Fed in some time.

Bolan reached his destination soon after. He parked his car, showed his identification at the holding facility's front desk and was ushered into an empty interrogation room. There, he sat down, but not before first checking the cameras mounted in the room and making sure they were disconnected. There would be no record of this meeting.

There was a knock on the door. Bolan told the visitors to enter. The two uniformed officers had between them a man in leg irons and handcuffs. He was wearing an orange jumpsuit. One of his fingers was in a padded aluminum splint.

Bill Griffith's face went white when he saw Bolan sitting before him.

"Sit down," Bolan said.

Griffith didn't move. He looked like he had seen a ghost. Bolan finally stood, grabbed him by the shoulder and pushed him the few shuffle-steps to the opposite chair. Then he pushed the man down into it and told him to remain there.

"C-C-Cooper," Griffith finally stammered.

"That's right," Bolan said, sitting down. "And you're probably wondering why I'm here." The Executioner reached into his pocket and produced a length of 550-pound paracord. He tossed it to Griffith. "Take that," Bolan said. "Put it in your pocket."

Griffith, numbly, did as he was told.

"It's a terrible thing that a crooked cop does, Griffith," Bolan said. "He betrays the trust of the community he is sworn to protect and serve. He betrays his family, who are shamed when his crimes are brought to light. He betrays his oaths. He betrays himself. A crooked cop is the worst sort of predator, because he can't even claim that he's true to his principles. He doesn't have any principles. He has nothing. He is nothing. He's better off dead."

Griffith turned red. "You look here," he said. "You can't talk to me like—"

Bolan reached out, grabbed the man's splinted finger and twisted. Griffith howled and almost turned a pale shade of green. "Shut up."

"Please," Griffith said. "Why are you doing this to me? You've won, haven't you?"

"I'm aware," Bolan said, "of how things work around here. Down here in Detroit, I mean. And I know you've had some visits from a law firm that, at least until recently, did some business with the late Reginald Chamblis."

"Yeah? So?"

"Have you given any thought to what will happen," Bolan said, "if you aren't convicted?"

"Why?" Griffith asked quietly.

"Because," Bolan said, leaning across the table. "if you don't go to prison for what you've done, the people I work with will throw you into a hole so dark, so deep, and so foul that it will make Gitmo look like a vacation in the Bahamas."

Griffith merely looked at him. The shamed detective's mouth opened and moved, like a fish out of water. No sound escaped.

Bolan stood. He gestured toward Griffith's pocket. "Remember that cord. I don't think there's enough there to use as a garrote." He shook his head. "Paracord's not really the right material for that, anyway. If you try, however—I mean really, really try—you just might manage to hang yourself with it. I suggest you consider it."

Bolan hit the buzzer. Someone came to let him out of the interrogation room. Griffith watched him go, looking shocked and dismayed. The soldier shot him a glance over one shoulder. "Think it over, 'Detective.' It would be best for everybody if you didn't go to trial."

The door closed behind him.

As he climbed back into his rental car, Bolan allowed himself to feel satisfaction. The mission had been a difficult one, as they so often were, but real work had been accomplished. Real good had been done. As he pointed the vehicle toward the airport, he rolled down the window, savoring the late autumn air.

It was just slightly less than a year until the next Devil's Night in Detroit. When it came, it would bring the usual vandalism, the usual arson, the usual predators hunting the usual prey. The city would be plunged into primal darkness. Rough men would be required to stand in the face of that darkness, to fight evil where it occurred.

For the moment, the Devil wasn't the most dangerous being walking the streets of the city.

That distinction went to Mack Bolan.

* * * * *